Kenneth S. Harris

Any Flavor Jellybeans but Black

Perkins May – 2015

Exterior cover design: Julie Butrymowicz

ISBN-13: 978-0692450321
ISBN-10: 0692450327

For Atticus and Cass, who will someday be 17 and confused, but completely unaware of it.

For Savannah, who is a constant ray of sunshine.

For Heather, who provides endless inspiration, an editor's eye and endless love for our family.

Any Flavor Jellybeans but Black

1

If I were a super hero, I think my name would be *Super Blood Man*. Or perhaps, *The Bleeder*! *Hemogoblin*? Not sure exactly.

But my super powers would be something along the lines of bleeding all over my foes until they become too squeamish to stand or maybe bleeding on the floor to create super dangerous slick spots in hopes that evil will simply trip.

In short, yes, I bleed. A lot. Far more than normal.

These days it seems there's only blood – blood when I sneeze, blood when I piss, blood when I shit – but specifically and especially, blood when I sneeze. It's getting to where I don't really think of bodily purges as normal colors anymore. No yellows, greens or browns. There's just red.

Maybe I'm exaggerating. But still, it's a terrible feeling to consistently see red.

Does this mean I'm dying? Well, if it does, then it's my little secret.

There's been an abundance of blood in my life since I can remember, though recently it's gotten much worse. Once when I was five, my Uncle Russ had me sitting on a thick concrete banister outside the church at my Aunt Winnie's wedding helping me tie my shoes. He had just finished up sneaker number one when I sneezed without the courtesy to cover my nose and blew a violent red spray across his forehead and balding scalp. I've decided since that it is essential that I cover my nose when I sneeze.

I'd like to say that I'm old and at the jumping off place with a fluffy white cloud or a bowl of boiling water beneath me, but that just isn't the truth.

After my morning dump, and taking extra care to clean the blood off my rear so it doesn't leave red streaks on my tidy-whiteys, I grab a checked over-shirt and my book bag and run off to school, skateboard in hand. What does that tell you about my age? I'm seventeen and just barely.

I've heard the philosophy before: live each day like it's your last. But I don't think I ever really understood it until I started leaking blood the way air conditioners condensate. On the way to school, I board without caution. Caution is for those with illustrious lives laid out before them, all the promises of tomorrow. I come upon Ailand Street, where I used to lose the board and walk – it's the steepest street between my house at 122 Olive and the high school – but not anymore. I brave the steep decline with daring precision, avoiding tiny cracks in the worn pavement and swaying from lane to lane just for the thrill of it. Close to the bottom, I ollie up and grind the edge of the sidewalk before tipping the nose of the board down and regaining position on the chalky concrete.

Before it's all over with, I want to try the Marty McFly trick from *Back to the Future*. You know, grabbing the bumper of a car and speeding along behind it, hunkering down so as not to be seen by the unsuspecting driver. Yeah, that's the coolest. I welcome speed. And you know, it's really working out for me. I haven't been late for school in nearly two weeks.

I arrive at school while the sun is just coming up. It's about 7:30. The buses are crowding the front entrance and kids are romping about. Most of these kids look the exact same to me. They could each walk through the same over-sized cookie cutter and fit perfectly.

Carly is sitting in the cafeteria having breakfast – she's the first thing I see when I walk in the building. I've heard people say that the world looks black and white, but just one special person shines in brilliant Technicolor. Well, Carly Henson is just the opposite. She emits the static hum of 1950s black and white television in an endless sea of high definition sitcoms. All around there's bright blue Nikes, glowing orange spaghetti strap tanks, designer jeans, even plastic, purple spec frames. Not that there's anything wrong with a little color. Hell no. Carly's just a little different is all. She's my best friend.

Carly was suspended once for her choice of apparel, namely, her black lipstick and dog chain necklaces. But that was in middle school. No one seems to mind here at Hemingford High School.

"Good morning, beautiful," I say, taking a seat across from her. I place my skateboard on the floor with my book bag sitting on top of it.

"Hey," she says, barely looking up from her oatmeal. Her hair is pulled back with just two curls dangling in front on each side of her face. "You eating this morning?"

I cast a cautious eye at the slop on her tray and shake my head no.

"Can't say I blame you," she says. "It beats no breakfast at all though." Which is what she was probably offered at home. Carly's dad will never win parent-of-the-year, and her mom died when she was just a kid. Around six or seven, I think. But her dad... Yeah, he sucks. There, I said it.

"If you say so," I laugh. "Say, have you seen Alan? I need some help with Chemistry. Big test this afternoon. I was up all night but I can't get it right."

"No, I haven't seen him this morning." Carly looks at me for the first time today. "Wow," she says, "I can tell you were up late. Your bags are packed, man."

I put my hands up to my eyes and feel the puffy circles beneath them.

"I've been having trouble sleeping lately."

"Me too," Carly says. "But it looks like you've got it worse than me. Take some sleeping pills. That's what I do."

She pushes the tray away and pulls out a plastic sandwich bag filled with tiny candies. My first thought is that they're an assortment of sleeping pills. Carly, for shame. But they're just jellybeans – and to my astonishment, they're all black. *Sweet-Annie*, my mom used to call them. Oh, how I loathe thee, Sweet-Annie.

She pulls a few from the bag, each candy matching her carefully painted fingernails, both black and glossy, reflecting the brilliant overhead lights of the cafeteria. She pops them into her mouth.

"You want one?" she asks.

"No thanks." I scrunch up my face and hold my breath. Even the smell of those vile beans from across the table is crowding my nostrils and invoking a sense of nausea deep in my gut.

"Come on," she says. "They're not that bad. It beats this crap." She inclines her head towards her tray, still half full.

"Can't stand 'em," I say. "Never could. My mom loves 'em though. Any other flavor and I could handle it. But not black."

Carly laughed. "Since when is black a flavor?"

"I don't know. Since some jackass invented those awful things."

She chomps down on another just to annoy me. I can't help but laugh. But when I take a deep breath, I don't dare use my nose.

***

When I was five years old, my Aunt Dolly passed away. She was as tough a woman as anyone has ever seen. Not afraid to speak her mind at all. At least, that's what I remember. Also, she was quick-witted, and quick to get pissed. She was the type who had already exploded by the time you noticed you'd accidentally lit the fuse.

I can remember her lying on her death bed, cancer eating away at her lungs, and she was still meaner than the devil with his tail caught in an elevator door.

My mother, Ruby, would say something to piss her off, and she would reply: "Ruby, you better hope I'm dead in the morning, 'cause if I'm not, I'm going to kick the shit out of you!" I can remember it like it was yesterday.

But despite the memories, I knew her as well as a five-year-old can know anyone. She was the first person I had ever known to die.

She had two children when she died: Kristina and Joseph. Joseph was a year older than me; Kristina a year younger. I don't recall either of them being very torn up about it. But even death looks so temporary when you're a kid. I wish it looked that way to me now.

What I remember most about that time is that everyone my mom knew brought food over to the house. There were sandwiches, pies, cakes, soups. You name it and the Guile house had it on that day. I didn't understand what was going on. Kristina, Joseph and I went on with our lives, or so it seemed. We played and ate the delicious food.

It seemed like a party to me, except some people were crying.

Like I said, temporary.

On the day of the burial, my mom was standing near the gates of the cemetery dressed all in her best funeral black. Her eyes were puffy and her cheeks were streaked with tears. When she saw me coming up the hill holding Aunt Winnie's hand, she tried her best to make it looked like nothing was wrong. But even kids catch on to things like that.

She held a little Ziploc bag of jellybeans in her hand. All black. Her favorite. She used to keep them in her purse at all times. She said they helped settle her stomach.

"Hey sweetie," she said. She knelt down next to me. "Are you okay?"

I nodded, but it seemed to frustrate her. In retrospect, I think she wanted me to be hurting. I think she wanted me to break down and cry and cling to her for dear life. That way she would have someone to comfort. Instead, I was the strong one. Or at least the ill-informed one. The one she wanted to be. Looking back, I think she wanted no knowledge of her sister's passing. Ignorance is bliss, or so the saying goes.

She went on.

"You know your Aunt Dolly is gone, right? She's gone to a better place."

"That's what Sissy told me," I said. Everybody I knew at age five referred to Aunt Winnie as Sissy. Everybody. "But wasn't she at the church this morning?"

My mom seemed annoyed by my ignorance. She huffed and sighed and sniffed and looked all around the cemetery. I didn't think so then, but now I think she simply didn't know how to handle the situation.

"You want some candy?" she finally asked and offered the bag of black beans to me. When all else fails and you don't know what to do with a kid, give him candy.

I took a tiny handful and ate them. I chewed quickly, as most children do when it comes to candy. But that flavor. That flavor ran over my tongue in a stream of vile bitterness that I can still remember to this day. It overtook my throat and then my nostrils until it was all I could taste or smell. It felt like I was breathing the flavor of black licorice instead of oxygen. Weird, huh? I held on as long as I could then spit the candy onto the ground and wiped the side of my mouth with my kid-sized suit sleeve. But no matter how much or how hard I wiped, I couldn't rid myself of the remnants of the taste.

I can picture myself now, standing there in the cemetery with my face scrunched up and black tar oozing from between my teeth. I felt like I had just eaten a handful of cockroaches.

"Aunt Dolly is gone the way Lady is gone," my mom said. "Remember when Lady died?" Lady was my first puppy. "Uncle Russ put her in the ground and you haven't seen her since. Right? Well, that's what happened to Aunt Dolly." She walked away with tears streaming down her face.

I can still remember when the casket was lowered into the ground. It was then, with that terrible taste still haunting my taste-buds, that I realized that what *used* to be Aunt Dolly was in the box. But *she* wasn't. It's a paradox that even now I only pretend to understand. Death is such a mystery, even to people who claim they understand it. At least, *I* think so. After realizing, I was able to cry with my mother. I now know that someday, I will be somewhere else too, while the thing that used to be me is in a box being covered with dirt while all the people who love me watch.

Every time I leave the bathroom, leaving bloody mounds of toilet paper behind, or sneeze a tissue solid red, I wish I could look death in the eye and say, "You're only temporary. You don't scare me." But instead I smell the faint odor of black jellybeans mixed with the stench of fresh blood that hangs heavy in the air, and then I think of how lonely it must be to die.

2

After school I meet Carly and Alan out front near the bus lanes. Alan usually rides the bus, even though most days Carly and I try to convince him to walk home with us. We hardly ever succeed. Alan's a chubby kid, and walking is not his forte. Well, if it is, he'll never know it, because he only does it when he absolutely has to.

I'm feeling pretty good this afternoon. Only one bloody shit at lunch time, so I'm feeling rather un-anemic.

"Carly tells me you need some help with your chemistry," Alan says when he sees me heading his way. The two of them are sitting on a bench on the sidewalk next to where buses file in to haul off kids.

"*Needed* help with Chemistry is a better way of saying it." I sit down next to Carly and sling a casual arm over her shoulder. "You're a little late, bub. Test was over two hours ago."

"Oh shit, man. I'm sorry," he says.

"Don't sweat it. It's just school." I grin devilishly. "Don't worry about punctuality. Now, if I needed help fixing my board—"

"Then you'd probably ask someone else," Alan says.

"Right you are!" I say. Carly laughs, covering her mouth with a pale hand with gleaming black fingernails. She always squints when she laughs.

We like to give Alan a hard time. He's much smarter than either of us – hell, maybe both of us put together – but we'd never let him know it.

I feel a sneeze coming on. I wince and try to hold it in. I know what comes with it, and here I am fresh out of hankies. I can't hold it any longer. My friends are talking but I barely hear what they're saying. Their words seem muffled by my effort to not spray blood all over them and the sidewalk.

The sneeze explodes. I cup my hands and sneeze into them. When I look at my palms it looks like I've been finger-painting a tomato patch. So much blood.

"Holy shit, Jace!" Carly gasps. "Are you okay?"

I look at her, imagining I look a lot like a clown with my big red nose. "Yeah, I'm fine. This just happens sometimes. That time of year, you know? Allergies and what not." I'm talking too much, well aware.

"Let's at least get you some tissues," she says. "Wait here. I'll be right back."

"You got it, babe." I pinch my nostrils together to hold back the flow. My voice sounds hollow and nasally.

Carly trots off into the school, leaving me with Alan who is gawking at me with an uneasy look on his face.

"Dude, are you sure you're okay? That's a lot of blood. You're still bleeding." Alan gets to his feet and I can swear he even gasps. I feel like I just informed my lover that I had an array of STDs mid-coitus. Alan, the lover in question, acts like I'm very contagious.

"Calm down, man," I manage to squeak out with my head tilted back. I face him; he slowly backs away, keeping a cautious eye on me. "Calm it, bro. I'm not going to bite you."

"Self preservation, pal," he says. "You should try it some time." But to my relief he is smiling.

Carly runs back with a wad of tissues. She stops at my side and presses a coarse tissue, as only one could find in a public school restroom or dangerous truck stop, to my nose. I pick another from her hand and begin mopping the blood off my clothes and chin. One thing I've learned since all this started, blood dries *really* fast.

***

Carly and I walk home alone, enduring the frosty breeze of a February afternoon. Once again, no Alan. Carly is bundled in a black suede jacket and lilac scarf. I'm wearing a thick striped hoodie, blue with a few dark stains on it from my little accident.

Carly seems a little off. She hasn't spoken a complete sentence to me since we left the school. She walks, but there's no bounce in her step; instead each foot scuffs the concrete one after the other. Her eyes are on the ground.

At last she says, "So, how long has this been happening?"

"What?" I try to play stupid. "Oh, you mean the nose, umm, the blood. Yeah. A few days. Nothing to worry about." Lie! Lie! Lie!

It's actually been happening my whole life, but never this bad. It's never really happened in public, usually in the privacy of my own bathroom, and usually no more than a trickle or a slight smear when I blow my nose. Now, it's been unrelenting for nearly a month. It got worse right after Christmas.

"Nothing to worry about? Are you crazy? You need to see a doctor!" She is nearly screaming at me. She looks at me with big bright eyes, blue like the ocean, though I've never seen it.

"I hate doctors, babe. You know that. Besides, it'll clear up in a little while. Just got to wait it out is all."

"I don't care for them, either. But if I were bleeding that profusely, I think I would have enough sense to realize I need medical attention."

"Carly, you're a girl," I smirk. "You bleed that profusely every month."

She thumps me in the back of the head. "Jackass! You know what I mean. This is serious! Don't make jokes."

"Okay. Okay. I'm sorry." I gaze off into the gray sky and rub my hands over my face and through my hair. I hate lying to Carly. But here goes.

"I'll tell you what. Give it a couple of weeks. If things aren't better by then, I'll see a doctor. Deal?"

Her eyes seem sad and pleading. She stops walking and grabs both my hands. "Swear?"

Damn it all. "I swear."

***

Carly has always been a bit of a klutz. I've known her since third grade and she was always the one to fall on the playground or tumble down the stairs. Once, she got her hair caught in a swivel fan and her dad had to cut it to get it out. Carly, the constant host of scraped knees and bruises.

In grade school and a little ways into middle school her knees were constantly scabbed, shins bruised, elbows scraped. Once in seventh grade, she even came to school with a black eye. She seems to have grown out of her clumsiness a bit now, but freshman year I remember seeing her with a busted lip, though she swore up and down they were just chapped – cracking and bleeding from the cold weather.

We walk by Carly's house first on the way home from school. It's a little weathered house on the corner of Willow and Burgess. We've been walking with our arms interlocked since I made my little deal. Which I may keep. Hell, I don't know. I would go, but you know... Fuck doctors. They don't seem to do people any good when they need it, and they charge you full price whether they heal you or not. Aah, the wonderful world of medicine – the place where no product has a definite price tag until after you already owe the cash. My mom's been paying medical bills her whole life and still hacks and coughs like she's the one who's dying.

Carly's dad's truck is in the driveway. It's a fairly new maroon Ford pick-up. It still looks nice except for a hefty dent in the driver's side fender. I swear, if the man would just give me a few hours alone with that thing, I could have that fender looking like new, minus a coat of paint of course. That could take a little more prep time.

"Call me if you keep menstruating out of your face?"

"You'll be the only one I call," I say.

"Sounds good."

She walks off but I call out to her. She turns to listen.

"Don't worry. Okay?" I say.

"No promises. But I'll try. You're my best friend, you know?"

Aww, Carly. I never knew you cared.

***

After leaving Carly's I hop on my board. It's cold, but oh well. As I pick up speed the wind stings my cheeks, ears and hands. It even nips at my chest through my hoodie. I suppose this thing is a little thin for winter, but it's only a few blocks until I'll be home.

Of course, the house is dark when I get there. No lights on anywhere. I suppose Mom is still at work. She's worked at the Hemingford Public Library since I was about 12. Before that, she was an assistant to the middle school librarian over at Nell Gilman. Weird thing is – my mom hates to read.

I hop off the board and take the spare key from beneath the wheel well of Malory. Allow me to introduce her, by the way. Malory is a pretty-going-on-beautiful 1983 Camaro Z-28 – red, at least in some places. I bought her last summer with money I saved from cutting grass and working part-time at Food City. Mom said I couldn't get my license until I had a car. So I bought a car. Then she said it has to run too, at least well enough to take the driver's test in. So, I've been sitting pretty on a learner's permit for going on two years.

Malory was in rough shape when I first bought her. I paid $1,000 cash, but I'd say I've put twice that into fixing her up. One day though, Mal. One day.

I take the key and unlock the front door then put it back beneath the wheel well. The house is depressingly empty. I make a sandwich and grab a bag of potato chips and head straight for my room, needlessly closing the door behind me. Mom probably won't be home until after 9 o'clock, so I flip open my laptop and play some *White Zombie*.

My cell phone spent the day at home since they are not allowed at school. I check it: no missed calls, no new texts. Just a high-def display of the time: 4:21.

Once the food is gone, I just lay back and take in the music, running through a full set of speakers hooked to my humble laptop, complete surround sound with sub-woofer. Killer jams, but for the life of me, I can't understand 10 words on the entire album – but one of them is definitely, "Yeah!"

Somewhere between "Devil man, Devil man!" and "More Human than Human!" I doze off, allowing Rob and the band to thump along in my dreams.

***

I wake to a persistent buzzing against the side of my leg. It's my cell, of course, but it doesn't register at first. In my head I'm thinking, *no, don't put that there. I'm a boy!*

To my relief, it's just a tiny screen glowing in the darkness informing me that "Alan is calling…"

"Hello," I say, still wearing all the signs of sleep.

"Hey man, just calling to check up on you."

"Ugh, why? I'm fine! Have you never had a bloody nose before? Don't you dare say no. I know better."

"Are you at a party or something?"

"What? No, why?" Now I notice that Rob and the band are still blaring in the background. I reach over to the desk and kill the music. "Just some tunes to nap to. Now, stop babysitting me. If I start to bleed out, I promise, I will call you, I will call Carly, and you both can come over and hold my hand through the whole process. Sound good?"

"Sounds amazing."

"I won't even charge admission."

Alan laughs his awkward little laugh, it almost sounds automated. A strenuous strand of "Ha Ha Ha."

"Say man, we still on for tomorrow night?" he asks.

"Why do you even have to ask? It's Friday, right?"

I glance out the window and see Mom's Cobalt in the driveway. She probably hasn't been home long or I would have heard from her about the roaring Zombie coming from my computer. Still, how long did I sleep? I glance at my phone while Alan isn't speaking: 9:12. Almost five hours. Damn.

3

"You know, I was thinking," Alan says as Carly and I join him on the corner of Ailand Street. "You could be a hemophiliac."

"Alan, that's crazy! I'm even a little hurt by that. I have nothing but the utmost respect for dead people."

He raises his eyebrows and peers at me over the top of his glasses.

"Just fuckin' with you, buddy," I say and punch him in the shoulder. "I've thought of that, actually, but I don't know *exactly* what being a hemophiliac means. I have an idea, but please, enlighten me."

"Hemophilia is a bleeding disorder in which your blood will not clot normally, meaning you'll bleed longer and more profusely if you get cut or something."

I swear the kid sounds like a professor.

"Hmm, perhaps that's it."

"So, what cut your nose and caused you to spray everywhere then?" Carly chimed in.

Leave it to Carly to put a damper on a good time. I simply shrug.

Every Friday night since we started high school, the three of us meet up and walk down to LC's service station – the only gas station for miles that still gives you the option of having someone else pump your gas – and get a 12-pack of RC Cola and a pack a smokes. None of us are 18, but LC doesn't give a fuck. The place also has a small garage on the side where you can get a tune up, a brake job, oil change, or a few other odds-and-ends repairs. I would love to work for LC, whom everybody calls Sugarman for some unknown reason.

LC's is only a few blocks away. It's one of the last businesses you'll see before the town gives way to winding two-lanes, farmland, and hollers.

LC himself is out front when we stroll up while the sun is still in the sky. He's under a silver Expedition with just his legs sticking out behind the front driver's side tire. I can hear a ratchet rattling from underneath.

"How goes the day, Sugarman?" I say, kneeling down next to the Expedition.

"That you, Jace?"

"Why don't you crawl out from under there and see for yourself?"

He grunts as he scoots out from under the vehicle. His face is streaked with grease and oil, his navy blue service station uniform is filthy. His thick head of hair is a fluffy gray, though now it's streaked with random lines of black from a hard day's work.

"Sounds like a smart ass, so I figured it was you," he says. I lend him a hand. He grabs it and I haul him to his feet. "What's it gonna be today? The usual?"

We follow him into the store. He takes his place behind the counter and grabs a pack of smokes from the wall and puts them down next to the register. Carly and Alan head for the back of the store to get some RCs from the cooler. I hang back to talk to LC.

"Yep, just the usual," I say. I pick up the American Spirits and begin packing them against the heel of my hand.

"When you kids gonna upgrade to Winston or Marlboro?" he asks. One corner of his mouth perks up in an awkward grin.

"Maybe once we're old enough to actually afford them," I say.

LC laughs and takes the 12-pack of RC Cola from Carly's hand as she and Alan approach the counter. He rings everything up.

"$7.24," he says.

"I know. Believe me, I have that number memorized."

We pay him and head for the door.

"Say, Sugarman," I say, turning around as an afterthought. "What would cause a fella to bleed all the time?"

He leans on the counter. "What the hell kind of question is that?"

"Just curious," I say.

He looks deep in thought, but for just a second or two. "My fist if you kids tell anybody I'm sellin' you smokes."

"Your secret is safe with me."

***

The three of us – the three amigos, three musketeers minus the muskets – head down the road a ways until town is far behind us. I can barely see LC's when I turn around. Up ahead there's a long bridge, and on the other side there's a tall sign for a railroad crossing standing just above an old set of tracks – two blinkers on each side. Those things go bat-shit crazy when there's a train coming. But now it's quiet. No sound, not a train in sight.

The bridge is an old rickety thing. I don't know how in the hell it holds cars as they cross. I'm afraid it's going to fall under just our weight. On the other side, the road crosses the tracks and curves away to the right, where the trees get thicker. If it wasn't the dead of winter the branches would be so thick it would nearly look like nighttime in there.

We come upon the tracks and hang a right. They lead down a straight path – old, cracked boards between shiny rails, large white gravels on either side. It reeks of mechanical industry.

The sun's about to go down and the sky is a depressing shade of blue, sort of like a bruise. I'm hauling the RCs and Carly has the smokes. She takes one out and lights it up and offers me the pack. I hand Alan the RCs and light up. I hand Alan the pack; as always, he declines.

"I can't understand why in the hell you guys do that," Alan says.

"Me either, really," Carly says. "It makes you feel good, I guess. Doesn't taste all that bad either once you're used to it"

"Come on, Al," I say. "You only live once, right?"

He dismisses me with a wave of his hand.

There's a place down the tracks a ways where we always hang out on a Friday night. It's behind a little diner that looks like it mostly deals with truck drivers and coal miners. It's so far down the tracks it's actually in the next county over, I suppose. Not sure though. We never go in and buy anything. We just take a little path out behind the place that leads down into a grove right beside Shelby Creek. We may hang out on the back porch occasionally, but not too often.

It's so goddamned cold. It feels like it could snow any minute. It gets colder as we head down the path and get closer to the creek. It's really bullshit that people call Shelby a creek. It's more like a river if you ask me. Wide enough to where I couldn't throw a rock and hit the other side.

When we get to our usual hangout, boy scout Alan takes off his pack and pulls out a tin of lighter fluid. He gets some branches together and puts them in the pit and coats them with it.

"Light it," he says.

Carly takes the cigarette lighter and touches the flame to the sticks and suddenly we have a small fire going.

We gather around the fire and crack into the RCs. Carly and I smoke cigs but Alan won't have any part of it.

"I'm thinking of getting my septum pierced," Carly says. "I think it would look killer, but my dad would probably kick my ass."

"Yeah, I don't think my mom would even notice if I got a piercing," I say. "We're never home at the same time long enough to notice each other."

"What about you, Al?" Carly says. "If you were going to get a piercing, what would it be?"

"I'm not sure I would want one," he says. Big surprise. "Maybe a tattoo though." Okay, surprise.

"A tattoo? For real?" I say. "No shit? What of?"

"Maybe a dragon wrapped around a sword," he says. "Maybe put a half-naked lady in there somewhere?"

"Cool. Some D&D shit," Carly says. "Think you'd ever go through with it?"

"Maybe. If I had the money."

I don't believe it for a second. It's cool to dream, I guess, but in reality Alan would never get a tattoo. His parents would flip shit first of all. Second, don't get me wrong, I love the guy, but Alan is a pussy. I can't count the times I've had to save him from getting his ass kicked at school. Alan is a favorite target for unsavories.

I don't say anything though, just nod and sip my cola.

Instead I say: "I hear Carly was about an inch or two away from fucking Jeff Rickman last weekend."

"Oh, what the fuck?" she says. "Who told you that?"

"That's just the word around the schoolyard," I say and take another swig.

"Well, it's bullshit," she says.

"Something had to have happened," Alan pipes in. "Rumors like that don't get started from nothing."

Carly shoots him a look of loathing. "I was at Samantha Jones' party. I was a little hammered, and Jeff came on to me. We started making out in the laundry room of all places. When the little prick tried to take my shirt off I came to my senses and put the brakes on. Told him to fuck off and I left. That's it."

I look at Alan. "Our little Carly is growing up."

"Fuck you!" she laughs. "What about you, Jace? Who's the unlucky lady in your life?"

"Easy now. No lady for me. I'm flying solo, as usual." I smile and light another cigarette.

"Can't seem to find one desperate enough?" Alan says.

"Al, buddy. I thought you were on my side, here."

"That's it," Carly says and launches to her feet. "I'm sick of all this talk. Let's do something awesome."

"Sounds good. Like what?" Alan says.

"I don't know. Something different."

I have an idea. It's different alright. Could be a little dangerous too.

"How about we sneak into the Anderson's backyard and go for a little dip in their hot tub?"

"Dude, seriously? You don't think they'll notice three half naked kids going for a dip in their backyard?"

"They probably would," I say. "If they were home."

"It's too cold for that," Carly says. And I can swear she looks a little nervous.

"Carly, the key word is *hot* tub. It's heated. Awesome in the winter! Let's do it!"

I pour what's left of my last RC on the fire and we all head for the Anderson's house.

***

Alan and I tip back the heavy lid to the hot tub. No cars in the drive way, all the lights off in the house, yet I'm still a little nervous. As soon as the lid is off, thick steam boils up into the cold night. I dip my hand in. To my chilled fingertips, the water is a few degrees past warm and working on hot.

I lose the coat and sling it to a plastic lawn chair sitting behind me. Next the shirt then pants. I scale the four tiny steps and ease into the hot water in just my boxers. Heavenly.

"Get your asses in here," I say and lean back against the side. Cold face, warm body. Pleasure is so confusing.

Alan sheds his thick Duke coat and awkwardly begins fumbling with his shirt. Alan's a fat kid, but he's not ashamed of it - at least not around me and Carly. At last his shirt comes off and his gut tumbles out over his jeans. He drops the pants, and so help me, the kid is wearing red briefs. I cast an astonished look at Carly, who is still standing fully dressed with her arms wrapped tight around herself.

"Alan," I say, "you look like the *Gerber* baby if he were dressed for a Christmas commercial."

He looks down at his choice of undergarment and says, "Fuck you, man." Then he scurries into the tub.

Carly is still standing there. So odd. I know she's not shy.

"Carly, what are you waiting for? The sun to shine?"

"I'm just not feeling up to it, Jace." She's looking at the big dark house, not at me.

"Oh come on, Alan and I have both seen you in your underwear more times than we can count. Hop in! The water feels awesome!"

"Yeah," Alan says, "me, Jace and about half the student body at Hemingford High."

"Shut up," she says. Alan just smirks it off. "I just don't want to. Now leave me alone."

"Carly, get your ass in this tub," I say. I even laugh when I say it, but she storms off all mad.

"Fuck you guys!"

The last word fades off and is more of an echo than anything. By God, she went home. She's gone, and here I sit alone in a hot tub with my tubby best friend. I didn't mean to piss her off. I was just playing.

"God, what's her problem?" Alan says. "Is it that time of the month?"

"You know Carly. If that was it, she would have told us. And then told us to fuck off. But I think she would have at least been nice about it. You don't think Jeff was rough with her or anything do you?"

"Not sure," Alan says. "He does have a bit of a tough-guy reputation."

"Well, if he did he's gonna be fucking sorry." I stare off into the darkness where she walked away.

"That's a hell of a conclusion to jump to," Alan says. "Maybe she was just cold. Maybe she was feeling a little sick. Could be anything really."

"Yeah, let's just let her blow off some steam and ask her about it tomorrow."

We chill for a while in the hot tub, bullshitting about school, girls, whatever. I'm staring at the sky, up into the bright street lights a few feet away on the other side of the Andersons' fence, when all of a sudden it starts to snow. Not much, just a flurry or two. It's sort of pretty, like the tiny stars that fleck the sky started falling all of a sudden.

"We may not have thought this through," Alan says, stirring me from my little daydream.

"Hmm?"

"We didn't bring towels."

We scurry from the Andersons' backyard, through the gate and into my yard, freezing our asses off the whole way. I bet we look so fucking stupid: two huddled boys with armfuls of clothes running about at night in the dead of winter — and in our underwear to boot.

Mom is home but it's sort of late so she's definitely conked out somewhere in the house. I grab the spare key and let us in. It's dark inside. At least Mom remembered to turn the lights off. She may have even made it to the bedroom this time. She's been known to get shitfaced drunk on a Friday night and pass out on the couch, kitchen table, sometimes even out on the patio. Again, she's an odd sort of librarian.

Alan and I rummage about in the washroom and come up with some clean towels. We shiver audibly and dry off. The repetitive jolt of my teeth rattling is unnerving.

"You want to just stay over tonight?" I ask him.

"Can't. I promised my mom I'd ride into town with her in the morning."

"Shit. It's late," I say.

"No worries. I can make it home. If Carly can do it, I can do it." He frowns. "You think she made it home okay?"

"What? Hell yes!" I say. "Carly's a big girl. Tough as nails too. She could kick your ass! She'll be fine."

"Yeah, no argument here," he laughs.

"I'll give you a lift home in Mal," I say.

"Dude, you don't even have a license."

"Yet I'm a great driver," I say. "Ironic, isn't it?"

I head to my room and change underwear. Poor Alan will be stuck in his wet briefs all the way home. He was right. We didn't really think this through at all. All in one shot, with one lousy idea, I managed to piss off Carly – somehow - possibly make Alan catch his death of cold, *and* I torment myself by seeing Alan in those tiny undershorts. What the fuck was I thinking?

No matter. This gives me a chance to drive, which is something I don't get to do nearly enough. I slide the keys from the rack on the kitchen wall. They look lonely — just an ignition key and a door key on a tiny silver ring. Thick black grips cover the heads of the rather small keys. We slip back out the door and I lock it behind us. I unlock the driver's side door of Mal, get in and reach across the seats to unlock the passenger's side door. The leather seat — freshly upholstered, thank you — is cold as hell against my ass. I can only imagine what it will be like for poor Alan with his damp trousers and all.

I put the key in the ignition and fire her up. She starts on the first crank. That's my girl! The engine rumbles and growls and for a moment I panic, scared shitless that it will wake up my mom. But then I remember, my mom could fall asleep in a time machine, go back to World War II and sleep right through Hiroshima and be none the wiser until she inexplicably woke up in Japan. I put Mal in reverse and ease out of the driveway.

I take it easy on the gas until we're well away from the house, and even then I don't press my luck. I've put lots of work into the old girl, but still, she doesn't get to stretch her legs very often. It doesn't take long for the engine to warm up and then the defroster is blowing warm air. Alan casts me a thankful glance.

Malory runs fine. She has for a while. There are just a few minor details that keep me from taking the license test. For one, the emergency brake doesn't exactly work all the time. Terrible, considering she's a five-speed. And there's something wrong with the rear passenger's signal light. I've changed the bulb and checked fuses but it still doesn't seem to work. Must be something in the wiring. I'll get around to it soon enough though. Sadly, I'm about out of money and it's the middle of the school year. It's sort of hard to find a place that will let you work two or three hours in the evening — even harder considering I can't drive myself to work. It limits my options considerably.

Luckily, there're not many cars on the streets. We roll up to the only stop light on the way to Alan's house, and wouldn't you know, it's red. I stop the car slowly and Mal sits there rumbling in the still night. The interior still needs some work. New leather seats but bare metal floors. Looks a little odd.

Neither of us speaks. We just sit there letting the car warm us up. Alan is rubbing his hands together over top of the vent that is pouring hot air onto the windshield. I see headlights in the rearview approaching. I nearly panic, thinking it could be a cop. But it's not. It pulls up next to me and I can see it's a newer model VW Jetta. Windows are blacked out, so for all I know it could be the Pope driving.

But Pope or not, the Jetta's engine revs high and purrs away back into silence.

"Is this guy for real?" I say.

I step on the gas and Malory growls at the car sitting next to us. I watch the dull-orange indicator dance across the numbers on the RPM gauge. I urge short bursts of fuel into the engine and – aside from the first blast – her RPMs never get above 2,500.

"Dude, what are you doing? You can't be serious," Alan says.

"Come on, man. You only live once, right?"

"You don't have a license, Jace! If you get caught you could lose the privilege to drive for the rest of your life! Maybe even go to jail."

"Yeah, and if I don't do it, then I could die tomorrow and never get the chance again. Hold on tight, man. And trust me."

The light turns green and I raise my foot from the clutch, feeling the power of the engine shift perfectly into the drive train. The back wheels spin out and Malory's ass sways back and forth on the asphalt like a graceful dancer. The Jetta gets ahead of me a little bit while Mal shows off her fancy footwork, but by the time I hit second gear I pass it with ease. Its nose is about even with my rear quarter panel. I push the engine to about 5,500 RPMs before shifting to third — one simple fluid motion between left foot and right foot, clutch and gas. Malory roars way ahead of the Jetta and I see the headlights dissipating into the dark behind me.

I look down and see that I'm pushing 70 in a 45 mile-per-hour speed zone and ease off the gas. The engine idles down and becomes a steady, deep growl, bubbly and smooth. Alan is as white as freshly bleached sheets.

"Dude, what the fuck was that?" he says.

"That was a Jetta. Didn't stand a chance against us." I grin and sling him a sideways glance.

"Not the car! You! You could have gotten us killed." He's screaming at me and I don't really care for it.

"I could've gotten us killed? On a straight stretch of one-way street? Dude, you can't be serious."

"I *am* serious, man. You don't even have a license!"

"Yeah, you said that already."

"Anything could have happened. That was fucking stupid."

"Nothing bad happened!" I say. "We're fine. Come on. You have to admit it was just a *little* fun. Just a little?"

He just looks at me over the top of glasses.

"Okay. I'm sorry," I say.

"Whatever."

"I mean it. I'm really sorry. I just wasn't thinking, I guess."

But truthfully I was — I was thinking about all the things I hadn't done yet, like running Mal wide open down the asphalt leaving all challengers in the dust, going to college, getting a real job, writing a book. Hell, come to think of it, I'd like to have sex before I die. Suddenly, I don't care for the thought of Carly fucking Jeff Rickman.

Man, this is fucked. And so am I.

4

Glorious Saturday morning! I wake up with the sun pouring in the window, the misleading devil. I know it's still cold as hell out there. It seems I've slept until almost noon. I got Princess Alan home around 12:30 and got back before 1. No trouble with any police or any troublemakers in VWs.

Alan worries too much. He needs to understand that cars make sense to me the way everything else makes sense to him.

But yes, sleeping in on a Saturday always feels so good. I sit up in bed and stretch and throw back the blanket. Carly is on my mind — I'm sure she got home okay, but still, I don't want her to be pissed at me.

I reach over to the nightstand and grab my phone and disconnect it from the charger. I turn it on and tap Carly's name on the tiny screen. The phone rings, and rings, and rings, and rings. No answer. Carly doesn't have a cell phone, so perhaps she and her dad are out. I call Alan instead. After a few rings, I remember him telling me he had plans with his mom, so I hang up figuring he'll call me back when he gets home. Sounds like an awesome Saturday ahead. Both my best friends are M.I.A. Whatever shall I do with myself? I turn on some music and crawl back beneath the covers, and oh so easily sleep takes me.

5

I wake up to the sound of my mom banging on the door.

"You okay?" she says. "You going to sleep all day?"

I glance at my phone: 2:07 in pretty white numbers.

"I'm not asleep," I say, stretching and yawning.

"Liar!" she says, but I hear her footsteps retreating down the hall.

I sit up in bed and slouch. As bad as I hate to lend myself to a boring day, I suppose I could get into something. There's been a welcome lack of blood in my life lately, at least in comparison to recent weeks, so maybe some boarding is in order.

Fuck my life. Spoke to soon. My pillow has a large red stain on it, collecting in a pool then pouring over the edge and onto my sheets — it's sort of the shape of Florida. I should probably run to the mirror in the bathroom and investigate, see how bad the damage is, but I just sort of sit there and look at it. I pick up the phone and tap Carly's name.

Again, it rings and rings, but no one picks up.

I decide to make the trek down the hall to the bathroom. The mirror is sort of dirty, flecked with tiny dots of tooth paste, saliva and God knows what else, but the rest of the room is spick and span. Blood is gathered and smeared and dried and caked all across my left cheek. The trail leaves my nose, transcends my upper lip, and finally plunges into a pool of red that covers most of the left side of my face and then leads down my neck. The neck of my shirt is hard and crusty with the stuff.

I feel a bit of panic. The ol' heart beat has sped up considerably. I even feel a bit light headed. I hear footsteps and slam the door shut and lock it. I tip my head down into the sink and turn on the cold water. I splash it up onto my face and rub at the stains. The water running from my face is red like a delightful summer Kool-Aid on a hot afternoon.

Once the stains are gone for the most part, I splash my face a few more times just for good measure and stare at myself. Without drifting my gaze, I reach for the toilet paper on the little spool and tear off a few squares and dab at my nose, wondering if fresh blood is still oozing out and if this could be it — the big check out time.

The tissue comes away clean. Thank God. I sit on the toilet with my head in my hands and contemplate running like a five-year-old down the hall and telling my mom everything. And her reaction would be to rush me to the emergency room so doctors can poke and prod me to no curative avail.

They sure as shit didn't do Aunt Winnie any good. She was like a mom to me. She was there when Aunt Dolly died. She practically helped raise me after my dad died. The woman was a saint. And doctors couldn't do shit for her.

Come to think of it, that's a lot of death. No wonder Mom is so bat-shit crazy.

I take a piss before leaving the bathroom — hoping and praying the whole time that the stream is only yellow — and then return to my room and put on some clean clothes, a sweatshirt and a hoodie, and grab my board and my cell phone. I put the phone in my jeans pocket and carry the board down the hall and to the kitchen. Mom is sitting at the table sipping something from a teacup. She's wearing sweats and a navy blue T-shirt.

"Look at you," she says. "The dead rises."

"Wha-what?"

She laughs. "You've nearly slept all day. I was expecting you to start stinking up the place any minute."

"Oh." I try to laugh, and at the very least, manage a smile. "You're not that lucky," I say. "Not today."

I walk over to the counter-top and open a half-eaten box of *Krispy Kremes*. I seek out the one that looks the most deadly — it's a great big custard-filled thing that's coated in chocolate with dark chocolate swirls and sprinkles. You can't die from clogged arteries if you bleed out at 17.

I take a big bite and turn to see Mom gawking at me.

"You got a little something," she flicks at her chin with her middle finger, "right about here."

I run my hand over my chin and come away with a massive glob of chocolate mixed with creamy yellow custard. The way the two colors swirl together reminds me of what it's like to sneeze blood. You can't really be sure where one ends and the other begins. I stuff the glob into my mouth and lick the remains off my fingers.

"Thanks," I say, but it comes out "fanks."

"Where are you off to?"

"Just going to do a little boarding around town," I say.

"With your little posse I bet?" she asks with a sneer.

"Umm, nope. Just me. Besides, I only think the board is big enough for one."

"You're such a comedian," she says, and then goes back to sipping the contents of the cup, which judging from the droop of her eyelids likely contains what's left over from her weekly Friday night binge. I leave her to it.

Don't get me wrong now. My mom is by no means a bad mother. She has her vices like us all, I suppose, but I wouldn't dare hold them against her. She just hasn't been the same since Aunt Winnie checked out. That's understandable I think.

***

I flip up my hood as soon as the brisk outdoor air hits me. The wind is bitter cold despite the bright shining sun overhead. I drop the board to the asphalt of the driveway and hop on, letting it coast down the small decline and onto the sidewalk. I kick at the ground a few times and pick up speed.

I smell something odd: the faint smell of iron and burnt wood crowding my nostrils. I sway back and forth absentmindedly as the board guides me along the sidewalk. There's an odd taste too — metallic with a hint of congestion and goobers. It's familiar, but has never been this intense. The sort of taste that would make even the fellas from *Jackass* retch instantly. I ignore it and board on.

***

I have never had an impure thought about Carly in my entire life. She's always been best friend numero uno. I suppose I've always sort of taken her presence for granted. Now that I can't reach her, it's eating at me. And now that I'm facing death, apparently with both hands tied behind my back, I'm regretting all those times I didn't have impure thoughts. Since I've been old enough to date, girls have come and girls have gone. But Carly has always been there. I've never really been serious about anyone — unless, of course, friendships count. Then you could say I've always been serious about Carly. And Alan. Oh man.

Once when I was in sixth grade, Carly and I were at Steven Sawyers' birthday party, which was semi-supervised. There was an impromptu game of spin the bottle on the back deck. It was dusk and about 11 kids were gathered around this tiny plastic patio table spinning an empty Pepsi bottle. This was before we became good friends with Alan. I don't even think he was at that party.

Anyway, Carly and I elbow our way into the crowd and two seconds later this bottle lands smack on me, spun by the illustrious seventh-grade beauty Natalie Parks. She was an adorable girl; one of her parents was from India, I believe. She got up and walked over to where I was standing and kissed my lips before I even knew what was happening. My eyes opened as wide as quarters and I grinned this big awkward grin. Everybody laughed — everybody except Carly. She didn't get pissed or anything. That's not her style. She just sort of looked at me and scoffed.

A few turns later Carly gave the bottle a spin and it landed on Steven. She practically ran to him and gave him this long, drawn out kiss, cradling his face in both her hands. I couldn't help laughing. I'd never seen anything like it. I think Carly got pissed that I was laughing. She went inside the house and was done with spin the bottle. She also didn't talk to me for the rest of the night.

A huge part of me wants to believe she kissed Steven so hard just to spite me, even though the thought had never occurred to me at the time. I was just into a good time with my good pal Carly, who had always been there, and as far as my young mind was concerned, always would. But now, with a constant concern of going to sleep and never waking up, I want her to want me. Yes sir, Cheap Trick. I want her to want me.

6

All it takes is one shriveled, disgusting chicken nugget to ruin the whole goddamned Happy Meal.

7

I get back before it's dark and give Mal a quick once over, double checking the oil, transmission fluid and the wiring that runs to the hot and cold posts of the battery. You see, she has this problem. Sometimes she just doesn't want to start. I get in and kick the clutch to the floor and crank the key and absolutely nothing happens. I cuss a lot and fuck around under the hood not really doing anything, then I try her again and she fires right up. No clue what's going on there, but I need to fix it.

Unfortunately, most of the things that remain wrong with the car, I don't really know shit about. I need to take some time and mess around with it. I think I can figure it out if I just put some time into it.

I blow the old girl a kiss and go inside just as the sun is going down. I check my phone, no missed calls. Mom is in the living room watching *House*. I drop inside and say hi.

"Hey," she says. "Dinner's in the microwave if you're hungry."

"Thanks, Mom"

Dinner is chicken casserole — not my favorite, but the price is right. I scoop some out onto a clean plate from the dish drainer and take it to my room. I settle in at my desk and shovel some of the gooey stuff into my mouth. I've never seen a chicken be such a hot mess.

I open the laptop and pop up an Internet browser and type in, "1983 camaro wiring tail lights," and hit enter. I'm sifting through the first few search results when my phone rings.

"Carly is calling…" it says.

My heart skips a couple beats I'm pretty sure and I damn near flip the chair trying to grab the phone from the bed. I tap *answer*.

"Hey babe," I say.

"Jace, can I come over for a little while?" she says. She's talking so quietly I barely make it out.

"Sure, you know where I live," I say. "You make it home okay last night?"

"Yeah, no problem. I'll see you in 10." She hangs up.

That was weird. I just sit and look at the phone for a minute, then toss it back onto the bed. I finish off dinner in a few labored bites and begin straightening my room up a bit. This is odd too. Typically I don't give a shit what it looks like in here when Carly comes over. I'll be damned. I have a crush.

I put all the dirty clothes in the wicker hamper at the foot of my bed, toss two empty soda cans into the trash, and run my empty dinner plate into the kitchen and put it in the sink. I return to my room and resume scanning search results, but it's no use. I can't really concentrate. I'm dying to talk to Carly. I guess this means she's not pissed at me anymore. But she *was* acting pretty weird on the phone.

But it's cool. I can wait… and patiently, I might add.

A few minutes pass and then I hear a knock at my door.

"It's open," I say.

The door opens and Carly steps inside, closing the door behind her. She just looks at me for a moment. Doesn't say a word.

"Hey," I squeak.

Still, she's just staring at me.

I stand up. "I'm really sorry about last night. I was just messing with you. Didn't mean to piss you off."

"Jace, shut up," she says. "I wasn't pissed at you. I'm still not."

She turns around and locks my bedroom door. She walks over and pulls the long red curtains closed. My throat clutches a couple of times and I nearly swallow Mr. Adams Apple when she grabs the seam at the bottom of her shirt and lifts it over her head in a fluid motion.

I've seen Carly in her underwear before and in bikinis and what not. We swim down at Shelby Creek every summer. It. Has. Never. Been. Weird. But now, I'm very close to horny. She's wearing a hunter green bra that seems even darker against her milky skin. Carly couldn't tan even if she wanted to. Her breasts are peeking up over the cups and swell as she breathes.

Holy shit. Down little fella.

But to my astonishment, she starts to cry.

"Hey hey hey," I say. "What's the matter?" Should I go to her side? It seems weird to hug her now. It shouldn't, but it does.

"I wasn't mad at you," she says.

"I know. I just thought because you ran off…"

She turns around and I see a series of savage marks on her back — long red welts mixed with puffy bruising and discoloration. It's the most color I've ever seen on Carly's skin. It's red, blue, black, purple, and a desperately painful shade of yellowish green. Her back looks like someone beat a rainbow to death and left it to die.

"Carly, what *is* that?"

"I just didn't want you all to see." She's still sobbing, hiding her face in her hands. As she slumps, her spine pokes up through the discoloration.

"What caused it?" My voice is a little unsteady now. My imagination is bouncing off all occurrences of wild. Was she mugged? Raped? Holy fuck me. Did Jeff do this?

"Did Jeff do this?" I say it without meaning to.

She begins shaking her head. "No!"

"Then what the…"

"My dad did it. All by himself. But his belt helped a little."

I just stare at the bruises and welts completely speechless.

I don't know what to do. My brain and body seem to be paralyzed. I just stand there and stare.

Probably needless to say, but I'll say it anyway: I'm fucking pissed.

I regain some use of my legs, though they feel tender and weak, like I've been sitting on them for hours. All tingly and what not, but they work, at least momentarily. I walk to Carly's side and place my hand on her shoulder. She starts a bit and turns to face me and wraps both her arms around me.

"I'm sorry I ran off last night," she says.

"Hey, that don't matter."

I hug her back and brush her hair out of her face. It's wet with tears. I tuck it behind her ears and stroke her head softly. Damn it. Damn it. Damn it.

My first thought is to drive over there immediately and beat the shit out of the guy. But let's be real, he'd probably beat my ass, or shoot me or something. He's always struck me as the type to own *a lot* of guns.

"How long has this been going on?" I say. "Is this the first time?"

"No," she says. Her head is buried in my chest so her voice is muffled. "It's been happening pretty much my whole life. But it got worse when mom died. And worse again since I got older."

My fists clench and I choke back down the idea of beating the man within an inch of his life. Try to stay calm. Try to stay calm. She needs you calm. Think.

"Well, it has to stop," I say. This seems to make her cry harder, which I don't understand at all.

I gently lift her head away from my chest and look at her eyes. They're soaked and her lashes, thick and black like her hair, are matted together. Her lips quiver a bit. I kiss her forehead.

"This has to stop," I repeat. "I won't let this keep happening to you. We should tell someone."

"I don't know," she says. "If we tell and then something happens and we can't prove it, I'm honestly afraid he'll kill me."

"We have to do something. Is he like this all the time?"

"Mostly when he drinks. Or when I piss him off."

Her sobs are slowly subsiding. I rub my hands up and down her arms as if trying to warm her.

"As soon as I'm 18, I'm so fucking out of there. I don't care where I go or what happens to me. I just want to be as far away from him as possible."

"You'll be 18 pretty soon, right?" I say. "Maybe we can get an apartment together or something."

Why did I say that? She looks at me for a moment and sniffs a few times.

"Yeah, that would be good," she says. "I'm scared shitless to go home. He seems to be getting worse. You know why he left those marks on my back? Because he heard that I fucked Jeff at that party."

I start to say something, but she adds quickly, "Which I didn't."

"I believe you," I say. "Anyway, that shit doesn't even matter. There's a psychopath in your house. The question is, 'what can we do about it?'"

"I'm just going to try to keep my head down and avoid him as much as possible until my birthday. I suppose if I'm going to move out soon I'll need a job."

"Yeah, me too," I say. "I bet LC will hire me for sure when school goes out."

"That's not until May though," she says. "My birthday is coming up in a few weeks."

"Then I'll make it work," I say. "Hell, mom may even let you stay here for a while. She's pretty cool like that." It's true, my mom never complains if I bring a girl over, go to my room and lock the door. Of course, a girl living here may be different. But we do have a spare room. Yeah, that could work.

"That would be cool," she says. "It would only be until graduation, you know."

"Yeah, then I'll be making bank working for Suga'man," I squeal in a high-pitched falsetto. This causes her to crack the first smile I've seen since yesterday. I return the smile and say, "It'll be okay. I promise."

I hug her tightly and it hits me. Son of a bitch. Now, I *can't* die. At least not until February 19th.

8

There's simply not enough time in the day for me to worry about all the shit that's on my mind. Carly left Saturday night around 10:30 and called me the next morning to let me know everything was okay, and that her dad didn't do anything ignorant. But man, Sunday flew by. I met up with Carly and Alan and the three of us meandered around town all day without anything to do. Just a simple, gray, cold, dreary, depressing Sunday.

I never knew a day could be so many things.

I'm boarding to school on Monday morning, not braving any steep hills, not trying stupid tricks that I can barely pull off. Point A to point B will do nicely. The thrill of the wind on my face is enough to satiate my need for danger.

I've pretty much pushed all fear of Carly's little problem from my mind — as best I can anyway. If I did nothing but worry about it all the time, I would just end up driving myself crazy. And a crazy Jace never helped anybody.

Instead of worrying, I've plotted and connived. We both need to be smart about this or things could go really wrong. Carly's plan to play nice should work well enough — just stay out of his way and hopefully nothing bad will happen. As for me, I can't just sit around and do nothing. I plan to go down to LC's after school and see if he can use me part time. It'll be tough with school and all, but I can make it work. LC pays pretty good for mechanic work. I should be able to save a pretty penny by the end of the school year. And I should be able to get my license soon too. The first little bit of money I get will go to fixing the last few things wrong with Malory – it shouldn't take much. Well, the money will buy the parts anyway; it's up to this guy to figure out what's wrong and how to fix it.

I could take it to a mechanic, but I wouldn't be able to look myself in the eye for God only knows how long.

When I get to school, the student parking lot is bustling with kids far more fortunate than me. They all have licenses — they're also not bleeding out.

The cold is starting to sting my eyes and I can sort of taste that foul flavor in the back of my throat. Does that mean the blood is coming back for another round? I can imagine the looks on everyone's faces — students and teachers alike — if I strolled into the building leaking like an antagonist from a Romero flick. Some would run away, some would run to my side. But I'm pretty sure they would all run somewhere.

I kick the board up into my hand and walk into the building, self-consciously checking my nose every few seconds. Still no blood. The cafeteria seems busy enough. Kids eating, talking, laughing, playing Magic: the Gathering. Now that looks like a game I could get into. The kids who play typically get picked on by... well, everyone, but I don't think I would mind. I'm pretty good at telling people to fuck off.

I scan the jumbled faces — it looks like all modern-day hits are playing this morning, but I don't see any classic '50s reruns. Where the fuck is Carly?

I start to sweat and my pulse starts pounding my veins. I should have called before I left the house... I think. If her dad had answered he may have gotten pissed and taken it out on Carly.

Damn it. I hate feeling like this. Afraid to call; afraid not to call. Stuck between a hellhole and a hard place.

Okay, my mind is made up. I glance at the large circular clock on the cafeteria wall. It's 7:43. If Carly isn't here by 7:50, I'm going over to her house. I'll walk right up to the door and knock... no pound... with my fist. Hell yeah.

"Hey." I hear her voice behind me, but just barely. I half expect to turn around and see her beaten to a pulp. But to my relief, the visible portions of her skin are as pearlescent as they were on Saturday.

"Hey. Everything go okay after you got home yesterday?"

"Yeah. It was fine. I just stayed in my room all night and read. Kept quiet. Didn't hear from him at all."

"Thank God."

She laughs. "God? Really, Jace? Are we in kindergarten again?"

"Hey, don't be like that," I say with a smile. "There is a God. And he's all up in this shit."

"You have such a way with faith."

"Faith is like peanut butter. Not enough and you can tell there's something missing. Too much of it, you're just going to make a sticky mess."

"What is wrong with you?" she scoffs and chuckles.

I feel a wet trickle on my upper lip. My nose just pissed itself. I dab at it with my fingers and look at the red on the tips. Carly's eyes are wide and concerned — that adorable bottom lip is puckered out really plump like.

"To tell you the truth, I have no idea."

9

The week passes easily enough, I suppose. I keep an eye on Carly, but not a close one. I don't want her to feel like I'm being weird or anything. I just want to make sure she's okay. And from what I can tell, she is.

On Wednesday, I walked her home from school, as is our custom, and her dad was outside messing around in the shed. I couldn't stop staring at the guy. He's around 40 or so I would say. He has sandy blonde hair, sort of shaggy and hanging below his ears, a thick mustache and prominent stubble all over his cheeks, chin and neck. He's not a fit man — probably around six feet and two inches tall with a bit of a gut on him. He has sturdy arms and legs from the looks of things. Yeah, he would kick my ass for sure.

I could tell Carly was getting nervous as soon as he came into sight.

She said, "Well, have a good evening. See you around at school."

I waved but kept on watching her dad. I would love to think that if things got really bad I could do something about it, but honestly, I would need a bat or something to clock him with. And he would deserve it.

Carly ran off and into the house and I watched the man raise his head from what he was doing and leer at her as she closed the door. My blood boiled, but luckily none leaked out.

But I let it go and just went on home. Besides, I didn't just so happen to have a bat with me. So, he was safe. Carly calls me a lot more now, which is very cool. I really enjoy talking to her. I feel like now that she's told me the fucked up shit that she's went through, we now share a special bond or something. I know it sounds lame, but it's really not.

It's Friday afternoon now, and I've decided when I meet up with the gang and we all trek down to LC's station, I'm going to see if we can work something out in the way of a job. It'll be easy enough, I think. I walk home with Carly anyway on a typical evening, then I can just hop on the trusty ol' board and speed on down to work. I can work from about 4:30 until 7:30 and can probably get a lot done in three hours.

Carly's dad wasn't anywhere to be seen when I walked to her house today, so I'm in better spirits. I just don't want to see the man.

I've got a little while before I meet up with Carly and Alan, so I've pulled Mal up on ramps and I'm underneath trying to figure out what's going on with the parking brake. The Internet says that in order to get the parking brake to work, I may need to replace the cables and calipers, and then adjust everything correctly. That sounds easy enough. I figure I'll mess around with the car and see if I can't figure it out. I have a little money. If it's not too much, I can probably pick up the parts while we're at LC's as well. This could turn out to be a pretty cool day.

I get a handle on what I think are the cables, but I should probably check the website one more time to be sure. This doesn't look too hard, thankfully.

I stop tinkering with it around 5:30 and go inside to get cleaned up after backing the car down off the ramps. I take extra care to get the grease out from under my nails and off my face using the hottest water I can stand, then I proceed to my room in a towel to put on some clean clothes. Underwear, jeans, T-shirt, hoodie. Ready to go, and early to boot. I fling myself down on the bed and grab my phone and give Carly's name a tap.

"Hello," a gruff voice says. Not Carly's voice. Well, not unless she has been hiding something other than bruises under her clothes.

At first I don't know what to say and after a while of silence, he repeats, "Hello?"

"Hi, Mr. Henson," I say. "May I speak to Carly?"

"Who is this?"

"My name is Jace Guile. I go to Carly's school. We may have met before when I was younger."

"Oh, I think I remember the name," he says. I was expecting him to be an asshole and accuse me of rape, pillage and plunder, but he almost sounds pleasant. "Are you the little boy that walks her home sometimes?"

"Yes sir," I say. I sound so fake and timid it makes me want to puke. "I really just walk *with* her since your all's house is on the way to mine."

"Ah, I see. Well, hold on a minute and I'll get her for you."

Well, that's a mind fuck. He was supposed to yell at me. Or at least be rude and obnoxious. I hear some scuffling in the background and some barely audible conversation, and then Carly picks up.

"Hey Jace. What's up?"

"I'd never talked to your dad before. That was weird," I say.

"Yeah. Was he alright?"

"Downright gentlemanly," I say.

"So… what's up?" she persists.

"Just thought I'd call before I come over. We still on for tonight?"

"Yep. But you don't have to call," she says. "Just let shit be normal. Okay?"

"Fair enough," I say. "I'm on my way."

"See you when you get here."

I hang up and leave and wonder if I did something wrong. Why must everything be so confusing?

**

It almost seems like Alan has been left on the outside this week. We haven't been intentionally ignoring him or anything, it's just that if Carly wants to talk about her dad or anything pertaining to that, we have to make an excuse to walk away from him. I hate it. I wish he was in on this too — partly because then I wouldn't be alone in knowing, and partly because we could include him in everything the way we always have. It just feels wrong to exclude Alan.

He hasn't said much since we all met up. No one really has. I break the silence.

"I think I'm going to ask Sugarman for a job," I say.

I'm on my skateboard, rolling along slowly, just kicking the ground once in a while when it feels like I'm coming to a stop.

"A job?" Alan says. "I'm not doing your homework. Not unless you pay me."

Homework. Right. I hadn't really thought about that. Oh well, grades are grades I suppose, and some people put a lot of stock in them. I am not one of those people.

"Why you want a job anyway?" Alan asks.

"I just figured it's about time I start using some of my God-given talents before I forget how."

"You can't forget how," Alan says. "You've been working on that junker so long, I figure you must be a master by now."

"Very funny, little man. You don't recall her being much of a junker the other night, do you? You know, when you were hiding in the floor board in the fetal position on the verge of tears. Does that ring a bell?"

"Wait. What happened?" Carly asks. She's been pretty quiet so far. I wonder what she's been thinking about.

"Jace, my knight in shining armor, broke a plethora of laws in order to get me home without having to walk in the cold," Alan says.

"You mean… that old thing actually runs well enough to drive?" Carly asks.

"Well, yeah, I just…"

"That's awesome, man! How long have you had it running?"

"Since about halfway through the summer."

"Why don't you have your license yet?" she asks.

"There are a couple of problems still. The wiring to one of the rear blinkers and the emergency brake don't work. I've been trying to fix them. They're just a little more technical than what I'm used to."

"Jace, I have to admit," she says, "I'm impressed. I didn't really think that thing would ever run."

She smiles and it looks pretty damned genuine. It's good to see her smile. She goes on:

"You must be really good with your hands."

What the hell? Really? Did she just come onto me? Or was she just fucking with me? I can't tell. I can't remember if maybe she's said something like that before and I always just laughed it off. I want her to be serious, but I'm afraid to pursue. She's pretty quiet again – just smiling and looking off down the street. Alan isn't saying anything either. He's watching his feet, almost like he didn't even hear.

"Yes. Yes, I am," I say.

Carly chuckles.

By the time we get to LC's station it's nearly dark. LC isn't outside today, but I can see him through the dusty front window lounging behind the counter reading a magazine. We walk inside. Carly and Alan head off to rummage the store while I approach the counter.

"It gonna be just the regular?" LC asks. "Pack of smokes? Maybe a lighter?"

"Just the pack of smokes," I say. "And an application if you're still looking for some help."

He looks up at me over his newspaper and grins.

"I ain't gonna lie," he says, putting the pack of smokes down on the counter and punching the price into the register. "Hearing you say that makes me happier than a pig in shit. Your mom okay with it?"

I hold up the smokes and say, "You really care what my mom's okay with?" I grin.

He laughs and rubs his face with his big greasy hands.

"You know me, Sugarman," I say. "I handle my own shit. My mom handles hers. That's how it's always been. Now, I need that job. You hiring?"

"Easy now, son," he says. "I know. I know. You finally trying to get that old Caramo running?"

"That old Camaro is already running, man," I say with a proud smirk. "Ask Alan how she runs."

"Aah, then what you hurtin' for a job for?"

I glance back at Carly. She and Alan are rummaging the coolers, likely looking for something other than RC. Sometimes they like to mix it up a bit. She looks so beautiful. Her hair is all loose and hanging down on her shoulders. She's wearing a brown leather jacket with dark brown fur around the collar over top of a Ramones T-shirt with faded dark blue jeans. Oh man, she's a sight for the sorest of eyes.

"Hey, Jace," LC says. "You still there, boy?"

I turn around. "Shit. Yeah, I'm here. My bad."

"You needin' money have anything to do with that little girl back there you're ogling?"

"What?" I can feel myself turning red. Damn it all. "I ain't ogling nobody! You're imagining shit."

"Well, if we can't be honest with each other, I guess I don't need to hire ya," he says with a wide sardonic grin. Fuck you, LC. Fuck you and the 180 horses you rode in on.

"Alright. Alright, man. If you're gonna get all red on me." I glance towards the back of the store to make sure Alan isn't within earshot to hear my half-truth. "We graduate in about four months and me and Carly are thinking about getting an apartment or something." Why must I be so damned bashful?

"You're already wanting to move out and be a man, huh?"

For a minute I think he's going to shoot me down, give me some sort of "you're too young" etc., etc. Then he says: "That's pretty good for a boy your age. You're good at what you do. So, I don't think you'll have any problem making a living or anything."

"Yeah, me either. And what I don't know, I'm pretty good at figuring out. So how about that application?"

"How about this?" he says. "Just show up for work Monday after school. I'll pay you under the table 'til you turn 18, then we'll fill out all the papers and stuff. That sound okay?"

"Hell yes!"

"You'll just be changing oil, flats, and stuff like that. Fixing the clunkers that come rolling in here. Fillin' up people's tanks, cleanin' windshields. But mostly I'll need you on the wrench. How's $12 an hour sound?"

"Sounds awesome!"

"What? $12 an hour?" Alan says. "You mean he gave you a job? Congrats, man."

For a minute I expect him to say something sarcastic or downright rude, but he pats me on the back and offers up a smile.

"Thanks."

Alan sits a six-pack of Grape Nehi down on the counter and looks at me and shrugs.

"I figure we could go for a change of pace for once."

"Sure thing, man," I say, and offer him a great big toothy grin.

I'm honestly so proud I'm about to bust. My first job! And $12 an hour ain't nothing to scoff at. That should be more than enough to get me and Carly a place. And I'm sure she'll get a job too once she's out from under her dad's overprotective, abusive wing. Yes sir, things are looking up.

We pick up our smokes and soda and head on down the road and towards the tracks. I look at Carly and she's smiling at the ground. I give her a play nudge with my shoulder and say:

"How about that? I got a job."

She looks at me. "That's awesome. I'm really happy for you." She reaches over and gives me a soft kiss on my cheek. Her lips are warm and soft and plump and wonderful.

"What the hell is going on?" Alan says. "You all have been acting weird all week. And I'm pretty sure, unless I've lost my mind and am now hallucinating, that she just kissed you. You just kissed him!"

I can't help but smile at him. I'm not really sure how Carly wants to handle this, so I'll let her take the lead. Besides, I'm too ignorantly happy to do anything effectively. She's just watching her feet and smiling all goofy like. Is that how I look?

"Alan, I've been meaning to tell you," she says. "Or, *we* have, I should say."

She looks at him and I find myself hanging on her every word.

"Tell me what?" he says.

"Jace and I are sort of an item."

What the fuck? Is she serious? Where was I when this happened? I'm so completely and utterly confused. She leans into me and throws an arm around my neck.

"Are you guys serious?" Alan says? "You're messing with me, right? Jace? Right?"

"Why? Would it be a problem if we weren't?" I say.

"Well, no. I guess not. We've just always been a trio," he says, and by God, he looks a little sad — a real sick, genuine sort of sad.

"If we were joking," Carly says, "would we do this?"

She takes my face in both her hands and kisses me hard. Her lips explode onto mine and they're all full and nice, and her tongue sways back and forth over my teeth. Why is this happening? I have no idea, but it's not like I mind. She keeps kissing me for a while, and I'm happy to kiss back. The kiss is sweet, but it stings. It tastes of black licorice – probably because it's plastered all over her lips in the form of lip gloss. But it's barely even noticeable compared to the pleasure the kiss brings.

When she finally lets go, I notice Alan is just standing there with his mouth open. I know it's just the light from overhead, but for just a second it looks like his glasses are fogged up.

"Ho-lee shit," he says. "So, I guess there's no chance in this being a polyamorous relationship, right?"

I just stare at him blankly, mostly because I have no clue what the fuck he just said.

"I didn't think so."

***

The night is bitter cold, and the little diner looks more like a crowded honkytonk. There's cars parked all around it and people standing out front smoking and more people laughing, talking and eating inside. We can see the place from a ways down the tracks, shining like a beacon in the distance.

The wind is blowing a bit, which only amplifies the bitter cold. I've got my arm around Carly and I love it — not just because she's the reigning object of my affection for all of 30 minutes or so, but also because she's added warmth. I hug her close to my side and our breath comes out like a thick fog and mingles together with the yellow lights from the diner. It's romantic in a very over-observant sort of way.

The three of us keep our heads down and pass by the diner hoping no one notices. Luckily, they don't. We head down the path and to our little nook. The cool air rolling in off the water is nearly unbearable. We rush to get a fire going and huddle around it. Carly and I snuggle up and I feel terrible for Alan. He has to sit there all cold and lonesome watching his two best friends snuggle without him. It must be excruciatingly weird.

The fire cracks and pops like dry ice tossed into a room temperature beverage.

"You know guys," I say, "we could start getting together at my house instead of down here by the creek."

"Yeah, we could," Alan says. "But what about tradition?"

"Good point. Tradition is important," I say. "Maybe we can start a tradition of catching the flu every year or something similar. Maybe even pneumonia!"

"Very funny, asshole."

Carly laughs and nuzzles her head into my neck. Her scalp is cold so I lean my cheek down onto it.

"Think your mom would mind?" she says.

"What? Y'all coming over? Not at all. We can just chill in my room or something. She probably won't even know we're there. She has her weekly date with Jack Daniels on Friday night."

I laugh a little bit at that, but no one else does. Awkward? Uh huh.

"So, how's your little problem been lately?" Alan asks, flicking his nose with his pointer finger.

"Oh, not too bad," I lie. "A drop or two here and there when I sneeze sometimes. Nothing major."

"That's good. Maybe it was just the change of seasons getting to you."

Here I could chime in about all the times I've shit blood — but truthfully that *has* subsided. I've experienced some sporadic nose bleeds in the past, but they've never been this frequent. For the sake of not worrying anyone — including myself — I don't rebut Alan's argument.

"Yeah, maybe it was."

I reach up to my nose almost instinctively, feeling my bare upper lip, searching for the familiar red stream. It would be hot to the touch right now since my skin is so cold. I pull my hand away and luckily there is nothing there.

We smoke cigs and drink purple pop for about an hour or so, and then I whip out the cell phone and check the time: 10:24. I lean close to Carly and whisper:

"What time do you need to be home in order to avoid Daddy dearest?"

She looks at me all awkward like. "Doesn't really matter, I don't think. He doesn't care how late I'm out. It could be midnight, or it could be 4:30 in the afternoon — if he's been drinking the two are one and the same."

"That's comforting," I say.

"Hey don't get all weird. You never worried about this shit before."

"Yeah, because I never knew anything about it."

She shoots me a sympathetic gaze, a quite pleasant one at that.

"Hey," Alan says. "Secrets don't make friends. Never have. Never will."

"Sorry man," I say. "Just whispering sweet somethings and what not."

"You mean sweet nothings?" Alan says.

"No. Sweet somethings. Why would anyone want to whisper nothing? You'd be better off not talking at all."

He opens his mouth to correct me, but I just grin devilishly. He closes his mouth and shakes his head.

***

When we finally decide to leave, it's around 11. The fire has burned down to just little orange embers and the night air is becoming unbearable. I go down to the creek and fill a Nehi bottle full of water from the bank, return and douse it on what's left of the fire. We get up and walk up the hill hugging ourselves. I'm hugging Carly too.

The little diner has died down a bit. There's only five or six cars in the parking lot and just two men standing outside smoking. It makes me wonder: Is this place a no smoking establishment? Why else would rednecks come outside to freeze their asses off to smoke?

We reach the top of the hill and make a sharp left onto the railroad tracks when we hear a voice.

"Hey kids! Y'all come back here for a minute." The voice is slurred and the words all come out in a gooey clump of phonemes: "Hey kiz! Y'all'ome'ack'ere ferminute."

We all stop where we stand, like the ground suddenly became so cold it held our feet fast to the dirt.

"Let's just keep going," Carly says.

I turn to look at Alan and he's standing there looking back at the owner of the gruff voice that just called to us. Now I find myself looking too. The man is standing beneath one of the outside lights to the diner so it is nearly impossible to make out his features, but he looks like a pretty stout fella.

"What you all doing out so late?" he says, translated from drunk-slur-speak to English.

"Just going for a midnight stroll," I say. "How about you?"

"I'm just having some grub and a little drink or two?" I can't tell due to lack of visibility, but I would like to think at this point the man holds up three or four fingers and looks at them completely dumbstruck.

"A stroll? You two fellers taking that little girl down to the creek?" He staggers forward and by God he looks familiar. "Your folks know where you are, girl?"

"Let's go!" Carly says. I'm inclined to agree. This man's oddly shaped yet stout form looks way too much like…

"Carly? Is that you?"

Shit.

"What the fuck are you doing out this late." His speech is somewhat more audible now as anger seeps into his voice. His rage seems to boost his words and give them a rough callused shell.

I turn to take a cue from Carly. I honestly don't know what to do. But she's running down the tracks and into the darkness. The man is approaching me and Alan with gigantic, determined strides.

"Alan, let's get the fuck out of here!"

But it's too late. He has me by the hood and yanks me to the ground with a single tug. I hit the wooden planks of the railroad track and the sky above me gets all blurry for a minute and spins around. Then I see his face, up close and angry, eyes drooping, but teeth clenched together in a ferocious snarl. He growls and spit sprays onto my face. At least it's warm. He pulls me to my feet by two handfuls of sweatshirt and then thumps me square in the nose with his fist.

I feel it instantly. The warm ooey gooey lava pours down my lips and chin. I can taste it, not just on my lips but at the back of my throat too. He hits me again and again. I hear Alan's voice screaming for him to stop, and somewhere in the background Carly is screaming bloody murder — no pun intended, and hopefully no foreshadowing either.

At last, he stops hitting me but I still hear his voice.

"Let me the fuck go! I'll kill that little bastard. Both of 'em!"

I look up to see two large men dragging him back towards the restaurant. I hope they're both sodomists.

Carly kneels next to me and I notice that my vision is a little fucked up, phasing in and out with my pulse like a light bulb with a bad short. I hear her sweet voice speak, timid and scared:

"Oh shit, Alan. The blood's not stopping."

10

Carly is right. The blood is flowing freely down my chin and dripping onto my clothes like water running from a faucet, though thankfully with very little pressure. I cup a hand over my nose but it's no use. I then cup both of them beneath my chin and watch them slowly fill up with thin red ooze.

"Oh my God," Alan says. He's backing up a bit. He never did like blood much.

Is this it? Shit. I don't really know what to do or think so I just sit here and keep catching blood in my hands and they run over and the liquid spills onto the cold ground with a sickening splat and seeing the puddle gather around me throws my pulse into overdrive. It's beating away in my veins and I can feel it powered by the commanding thump of my terrified heart. *Breathe.*

"We have to get him to a doctor," I hear Carly say. "Alan, what the hell is happening?"

"Oh God! Oh shit! I don't know."

I don't even bother getting to my feet. My vision is still way off doing that weird pulse thing. My hands are shaking and I drop them to my sides allowing the mess of red to spill to the ground with a sickening splat. I feel hands on me, tucking beneath my arms and pulling at me to no productive end.

"Alan, get your ass over here and help me!" I hear Carly scream. "Alan, now!"

I look up and see him quite a few feet away from me acting like he wants to walk over and help, but he's crying and shaking and I don't think he'll be able to. I think he knows it too.

"Here, tilt your head back," Carly says. Her voice is weak and uneven yet reassuring. She places a trembling hand beneath my chin and the other on my forehead and lifts my head back.

A few trickles run down the sides of my cheeks and I feel fresh blood on my neck. Carly pulls a pair of purple gloves from her pocket and places one over my nose. It feels comforting for a moment, like it's easily holding back the flow — after all, no water pressure, right? I stare up at the night sky. It's all black and empty and threatening yet oddly serene.

But something strange is happening. I feel Carly's breath on my cheek and taste that awful metallic flavor in the back of my throat. I smell blood and I swear to the lord up above and the devil down below that there's a faint stench of sweet-Annie. I begin to cough and wretch and gag. I feel a thickness in my throat and a particularly hoarse cough spews a mixture of blood and saliva onto the ground. The pain seers hot from nose to throat, from throat to teeth and lips. I crawl onto my hands and knees and collapse to my side and just lay there.

"Alan, come on!"

Now they both have me, one under each arm, and they're hauling me to my feet. With both of them hoisting, the plan works. They hobble down the train tracks with my weight on their shoulders. It's such a long walk, I actually feel bad for them. But damn it all. I'm dying! I don't know whether to pray or curse. I wonder if it's ever okay to do both.

The walk seems to take forever. Luckily, the blood is back to flowing on the outside, though that terrible taste is still dominating my mouth and throat. I seem to taste it all the way into my chest — blood, metal and bile. I imagine I look like a big-screen zombie with really talented make-up artists. I'm so dizzy. The ground is bouncing all around me and the road in the distance could be on another planet for all I know. It's down in the dirt, then up in the air, then over in the trees. It's everywhere all at once.

"Jace, hold on!" Carly says. "We'll get you to a hospital or something. Maybe Sugarman's still at the station. That's not too far. You'll be fine. I promise."

She's crying while she talks.

Eventually we get to the road. Our feet haven't been on the blacktop for more than two minutes when Carly's knees buckle and I pitch forward and fall to the ground. I lay and squeeze my eyes shut, then release.

"Shit!" she says. "Are you okay? Are you okay?"

"I'm alright," I say. I hold my sleeve up to my nose and roll onto my side. The ground is painfully cold, even through my layers of clothing. I feel so weak, like I couldn't lift a pencil to sign a contract for my soul. Shit, pen. Pen, definitely pen. You can't sign contracts in pencil.

"I'm going to run and check to see if Sugarman is still around," Alan says. "He's probably gone, but it's worth a shot."

I watch him run off into the distance. His run is weird, more of a jostle from foot to foot. Very little arm movement. He would never walk a tight rope. That's for sure. But maybe he can build computers for a living. Yeah, Alan'll be alright. Computers are only increasing in popularity. That's a solid future.

I hear Alan screaming obscenities. I can just barely see him in the darkness, smacking Sugarman's door with his chubby little hands. I take it no one is home at the service station. I lie back on the cold blacktop and give in. Fading, fading, gone.

11

I wake up and see ankles. Three pairs of ankles in tight fitting black jeans, nude panty hose, and loose khakis. I recognize some of these ankles, but the nude panty hose... Their owner is evading me. Who could this person be? I look up and see an older lady — I wouldn't say elderly by any means — looking down at me and smiling.

"Looks like he's coming around," she says. "Here, help me get him onto the couch. The bleeding seems to have stopped."

I feel awkward, chubby hands beneath my arm pits and I'm suddenly hoisted to my feet. I feel the ground beneath them and try hard to make my legs solidify. They take hold but wobble beneath my weight and Alan's hands grasp my sides. Oh those old familiar chubby hands. I mean that in the most heterosexual way possible.

"Careful with him. Oh my God!" It's Carly's voice. I'd know it anywhere. Sweet, sweet Carly and her wonderful voice coming from between the world's most beautiful lips. Suddenly the world around me turns topsy turvy again and I feel fluffy cushions on my back.

"Fluff this up and put it under his head," the lady says. She's wearing a denim skirt and lime green blouse. I love lime green. I've decided this lady is A-Okay with me.

Carly's familiar hands hold my head while someone places a glorious pillow beneath my throbbing skull. You never know what you're thankful for until it props your head up. That doesn't make sense. Oh well. A lot doesn't make sense right now. Where the hell am I?

"Where the hell am I?" I say. Yes sir, thinking out loud again. Or madam. Sorry.

I lift my hand to my upper lip and rub it. My hand is heavy and feels three times its normal size and my upper lip is crusty with drying blood. I feel the urge to panic, but really there is no need. After all, *drying* blood is the important detail. Neither a river, nor even a stream, turns crusty 'til it ceases to flow and remains perfectly still. Goddamn, I'm a poet. A poet minus a nosebleed which is more than I could have said however long ago. Wait, how long have I been out?

"Take it easy now boy," the lady says.

"Just lay back, man." That one is Alan.

I lift my head, which feels like a dumbbell at the end of my neck. So much weight. I turn my head slightly and take in the surroundings. There's a window and outside it's pitch black with just a few street lights shining down. It must still be night, or a full day later, or even a few days later. Who's counting? Definitely not me.

"You're in my house," says the lady. "My name is Charlotte Wills."

"Why didn't you take me to the hospital?" I say, a little shocked at myself considering my loathing of doctors, nurses, surgeons, etc.

"You had lost a lot of blood," she says. "And my house was closer. And I am a nurse. I figured I'd bring you here and do my best and call an ambulance if need be."

"No ambulance," I say. "I'm fine."

"No ambulance? Son, have you seen yourself? I thought you were dead when I saw you on the side of the road. We'd just got you through the door when you started to come around."

"I hate doctors," I say. In my head my voice sounds stern, but when it comes out it's weak and puny and I'm sort of ashamed to use it in front of my dear sweet Carly. Carly...

"Carly, are you okay?" I ask, remembering her dad was the reason all this began.

"I'm fine," she says. "Don't worry about me. Let's just get you taken care of."

I lift my head up and seek her out. Her eyes are wet and her face is red. Her hair is matted to her cheek in a stream of tears. She's still bundled in her coat and hugging herself as if cold, even though the temperature in this house is soaring.

The house looks nice enough I suppose. It's well-kept and tidy. You can tell this lady cleans a lot, probably has a family stashed away somewhere. There are pictures on the walls of her and a bald man of around the same age, and some of a younger girl, probably around 19 or 20. Blonde hair, really hot. Not as hot as my Carly though. No, not my Carly. That's possessive and weird. Carly, woman of the future, amazing female specimen who makes everyone who knows her proud. Indeed.

"Here, sit up a bit," Charlotte says. "Drink this."

She hands me a cup of cool liquid. I drink it without question and not knowing what to expect. Bland, tasteless, but very cold. Just water. Sweet, refreshing, wonderful, soothing water. I drink it quickly and it mingles with the taste of blood in my mouth and on my lips and I feel the fiendish mix run down my throat and to my stomach where it sits and turns and twists. I may puke. Damn it, I hope not.

I force myself to sit up on the couch and reach the cup back to Charlotte. She takes it and asks, "Would you like some more?"

"No thanks," I say.

Carly comes to my side and wraps her arms around me.

"Damn it, you scared me to death," she says. Her arms squeeze me and for a moment I feel like I may break.

I want to tell her to loosen up a bit, but I can't. Carly's embrace is too important for me to ever turn away. How does the old saying go? *Grin and bear it.*

Charlotte leaves the room. I see her denim skirt swishing around the corner over Carly's shoulder.

"Dude. You need to see a doctor," Alan whispers.

"Why? Because some douche bag punched me?" I look at Carly from the corner of my eye. "Sorry. Him being your dad and all."

"No offense taken."

"No," Alan says. "Not because you got punched. Because you bled for like an hour *after* getting punched. Copious amounts too. That means a lot in case you didn't know. Plain and simple, you bleed too much – way too much – and you need to see a doctor before something terrible happens. Well, more terrible than this. And this is pretty fucking terrible, Jace."

"Easy, Dad," I say. "Calm down. I'm fine. Dude got in a lucky shot and that's it." I flip the collar of my coat and try to act cool though I feel like hell warmed over. Shit, that's redundant. I don't feel good.

"I stand by what I said, Jace. You need a doctor." His voice is still low and raspy.

Charlotte comes back into the room carrying a blue plastic tub of water and a wash cloth. She sits the pan next to the couch and kneels beside me, dipping the rag into the water and then ringing it out vigorously.

"Lay back," she says. "Lay back and let's get you cleaned up a little. How are you feeling?"

"I'm a little light in the head," I say. "But I'm fine for the most part. I'll just walk it off and everything will be okay."

"I still think I should call you an ambulance," she says, and dabs the damp rag against my face, all along my lips, chin and cheek. The water is cool and it feels like heaven.

"No, please ma'am," I say. "I appreciate everything that you're doing for me, but I really don't care for doctors and hospitals."

"Now, why is that?" she asks. "What could doctors possibly do that is so bad? They can help you, you know?"

"I don't think so," I say. Don't get angry, Jacey ol' boy. Don't get angry. "Doctors and surgeons and nurses didn't do shit for my aunt. They told us all she was going to pull through, no problem. But guess what? There was a fucking problem. A *big* fucking problem, because she's dead now. But I guess they don't give a shit because they still got their payday."

Her eyes are wide and she's looking down at me and dabbing away.

"You sure have a mouth on you," she says. "What's your name?"

"Harvey," I say.

Alan looks at me like I just offered the Pope a 10 inch dildo named Chester. Yes, Alan, I lied. So, sue me. The last thing I need is this do-gooder nurse to call my mom and inform her of my little problem. Anyway, haven't we always said, (though in regards to women) never trust anything that bleeds for days at a time and doesn't die? That's right, sir.

I shoot Alan a look that clearly says, "Shut your mouth or I'll shut it for you."

He shuts it.

"Well, Harvey," do-gooder nurse Charlotte says. "Why don't we call your mom and get her to come pick you up? What's her number?"

That's it! I spring to my feet, swinging my legs over the side of the couch. My left foot lands square in the pan of cool water previously being used to dab dried blood from my face. It's cold and nice in a way, but damn it all I'm pissed.

"Listen, Charlotte," I say, a little hostile in spite of my best efforts not to be. "Thank you for your help, for not leaving me in the middle of the road to bleed to death. I do really, sincerely appreciate the effort. But I'll thank you not to pry, and not to push your good intentions on me. Thank you."

I walk away, ignoring the indignant looks from my companions. They can follow or they can stay behind and tell all my secrets. Harvey's secrets. Jace's secrets. I'm so angry at the moment, I really don't care. I see a door and I'm heading for it.

Outside the night air is freezing. I walk out onto the porch and descend the stairs and stand hugging myself at the bottom and feeling guilty for the way I spoke to the kind stranger. I hear the door open and light footsteps patter across the wooden planks. I turn to look. It's Carly. Good ol' faithful Carly.

"Hey," she says. "It's cool. Just calm down."

She puts her hands on my shoulders and I take her into my arms. She's so warm. I hug her tightly to my chest and wrap the ends of my coat around her. I swear, if I could I would zip up this coat and spend an awkward eternity inside a coat with her.

I can see my breath over her shoulder. It's thick and white like cigarette smoke and comes out in long streams as I deliberately exhale with extra force. The door opens again and I can see Alan standing at the top of the stairs. I wonder just how much he told the good nurse. I look at him sternly, feeling no need or desire to apologize. No sir, Alan. Just follow my lead, man. Come on! We've been running this race since seventh grade. I just go on hugging Carly and thanking my lucky stars that I'm still alive and that I have her and that she is safe.

"I'm sorry, man," Alan says. "I was just worried about you. I didn't mean to piss you off."

I ease my embrace around Carly's frame for a moment and motion for him to come down the steps. He does, like a good boy. I sidestep Carly and meet him and stand toe to toe with him, and for a moment I'm shocked that I'm actually thinking about hitting the poor kid. Me? The guy who has always played the savior for Alan. Me, hitting him in the face to teach him a lesson? I don't think so. I've saved his ass one too many times for me to start pounding on him. I could have started years ago and been one of the popular assholes at school.

I slap him on the shoulder playfully and say, "No worries, man. We're good. You tell my secret?"

"No, I just said I was sorry and left," he says nervously.

"Good," I say, and smile at him. "Now, let's all get the hell out of here."

We walk away from Charlotte's house and towards a tiny paved road that runs in front of what looks like a corn field. Of course, it's hard to be certain in the winter time. For a moment, I feel like I may panic because I honestly have no clue where I am. I look around and see trees and mountains and a barren field, a farm house or two and a one-lane paved roadway that doesn't look like it leads to much in either direction. I rub my forehead and think hard and gaze down the lane, one way and then the other. Aah, yes! Crystal Creek Road! Damn it all!

"We're a long way from home," I say. "It'll probably take us the better part of three or four hours if we hoof it. What time is it?" I ask rhetorically and pull my cell phone out of my jeans pocket before the sentence is even out of my mouth. It's 12:15 and ticking.

"Holy fuck," Carly says. "My dad is going to kill me." Her lips quiver as she speaks.

I put my fingers beneath her chin and tilt her face up to mine. "Like hell he is," I say. "This shit is real close to personal. He won't hurt you. I swear."

She smiles, but just barely, and plants a soft kiss on my cheek. "My hero," she says. "My wondrous, bloody hero."

Hemogoblin?

"You know it," I say. "So, three or four hours is definitely out of the question. Who's up for a little hitchhiking?"

12

"Hitchhiking, dude?" Alan screams as we walk the one-lane blacktop. "You've got to be joking! Not even *you* can be that stupid."

"I'm not stupid, Alan," I say. "And you know it. We have to get home quick and this is the only way. Besides, whatever happens, I can handle it. Just trust me, man."

"Oh, you mean the way you handled Carly's dad? My hero!" He mocks Carly and bats his eyes with emphasis.

"Hey asshole! Watch your mouth." I'm seriously rethinking my decision to not hit him. Just stay calm. Stay calm.

"Jace, this has just been a terrible night and I want it to be over without any more bad shit happening." He stops dead in his tracks and runs his hands through his hair. "Can't you just call your mom or something?"

I know the area, so I whip out my cell phone with confidence. There isn't any signal anywhere outside the city limits. Everybody knows that.

"Look!" I say, and flash him the brilliantly lit screen, glowing like a firefly in the darkness. "No signal. You know better than that. Do you even know where we are?"

"No, not really," he admits and I can tell he looks a little scared and coming up on terrified. He is shaking and his eyes look glassy and wet beneath his thick glasses. I feel for the guy, I really do. But damn it, if he would just listen to me everything will be okay.

"Well, we're way out in the fucking boonies, man. Trust me. There are some bad folks who live around here."

"Yeah, and you want to catch a ride with one of 'em!"

"Just trust me!" I shout. "Please!"

"Guys," Carly says and steps between us. "Calm it down. Screaming at each other isn't solving anything. Just be cool."

"We haven't heard from you yet," Alan says. "What do you think, Carly?"

She doesn't even miss a beat. "I think we should trust Jace. He knows what he's doing."

"Really?" Alan says. "Awesome. Ever since you two started fucking I've been the odd man out."

I snap. I can't take this bullshit anymore. I grab Alan by the collar of his jacket and drag him to the side of the road and slam his back against a tree. He looks at me in terror and he's whimpering like a beat dog. His hands push on my chest but it's no use.

"Watch what you say, Alan," I say. "Please. You know you're my friend and I love you like a brother. But do *not* talk about her that way. I won't put up with that. Not from you."

"I'm—I'm—I'm sorry," Alan squeaks. "I was just angry. You know I love you guys. I've just felt so left out lately. I didn't mean—mean any disrespect. I was just talking but not thinking. Come on. You know I didn't mean it."

I loosen my grip and turn to face Carly who is still standing in the road with her hands cupped over her mouth and her eyes wide. She runs to my side and puts her arms around me and Alan. The three of us, three amigos if ever there were, stand here in the cold and huddle together and Carly cries and Alan cries and I just gaze about confused for a moment, and then I'll be damned if a single tear doesn't leak out of my left eye followed by a steady flow from both.

This goes on for a while and I hug back tightly and am thankful to have friends who give a shit, and then we all agree to trust good ol' Jace — Jace who will not lead us astray — to hike out to the main road and try to hitch a lift, hopefully with a nice-looking lady or cleanly shaved fellow, but more than likely a large, surly trucker.

We trek on out of Crystal Creek and to the main road. It only takes about 10 minutes or so and then we are on two-lane blacktop as opposed to one-lane. The road is beaten and worn in several places. And every few steps I spot a large chug hole that looks like if a car were to hit it the tire would surely burst. Five minutes or so pass and we are met with no cars. Just be patient, everyone. A car will come.

And sure enough, there it is. Headlights in the distance come around a curve and damn near blind us all. I raise my hand up to shield my eyes and pull my friends to the side of the road as though they're not smart enough to get out of the road on their own. Sorry guys. I mean no disrespect.

Once safely out of the road, I lift a hand in the air, thumb up. The car, a beat up late-90s model sedan, passes right on by without even braking. I look at Carly and then Alan and they both look discouraged.

"It's cool, guys. Nobody gets it on the first shot," I say.

It'd be just our luck if it started to rain. If this were a cheesy movie it certainly would. But the night looks clear as crystal up above us. A perfect night for a drive – hear me, random stranger? That's your cue.

We're on the road another few minutes. No one speaks. There is no sound except for the occasional cricket and the scuff of our shoes on the blacktop.

The next vehicle approaches and I step forward, both feet on the road and well past the white line. The tiny hatchback swings wide and into the other lane to keep from hitting me, but then slows and eventually stops another hundred feet or so up the road. I shoot Carly and Alan a cautious look and say, "wait here," before running towards the stopped vehicle. I got important details along the way: it's a Ford Focus, newer model, and most importantly, it's out of state.

The most important skill for hitchhiking is being a good judge of character. I mean, you don't have to be able to tell a person's favorite kind of breakfast cereal, just whether or not they're going to kill, rape, maim or otherwise cause bodily harm to you or your entourage. I feel I'm pretty good at it, seeing as I'm still alive.

I'm relieved to look inside the tiny hatchback – it's maroon, though it looked black at a distance – and see a middle aged woman wearing thin-rimmed specs, sweat pants and a faded blue UNC sweatshirt. Some Jesus-on-a-cross air freshener hangs from the rearview, making the whole car smell like sweet salvation.

She looks at me over the top of her specs and says, "What in good gracious happened to you? You don't look so well."

"I got beat up and left on the side of the road. My friends back there pretty much saved my life."

She looked in the rearview, probably trying to get a look at Carly and Alan.

"My name is Harvey," I say and put my hand in through the open window. She shakes it a bit cautiously.

"Emily," she says.

"I'm really sorry to bother you, and I know hitchhiking is a terrible idea. I'm just trying to help my friends get home," I persist. "It's late and they're probably going to be in trouble. And all because they helped me out."

She glances about from me to the rearview to the cellphone in her cup holder.

"Well, I can't leave you standing out here. I wouldn't sleep a wink tonight."

"You're a life saver," I say.

I motion for Carly and Alan to join me, then open the passenger's side door and climb in. I feel a little guilty for that crack about not trusting anything that bleeds for five days and doesn't die. If this had been a man decked out in Jesus, I may have been hesitant to climb in, thinking the religious décor is a clever ruse to trap young folks into getting in his car. But I got no such vibes from Emily.

Instead I get in, lean back and let the smell of sweet salvation wash over me.

***

The drive is pleasant, though no one says much. The car hums and the radio whispers standard pop hits, one after another.

After careful consideration, I get Emily to drop us off about two blocks from Carly's. It's more important for her to get home earlier than me and Alan. We may get scolded or grounded, but Carly may get her ass beat.

Emily pulls over to the curb and comes to a complete stop. "Here?" she says.

"Yep, this is good," I say. I open the door to get out but I feel another twinge of guilt. I look at Emily and say, "I have a confession. My name isn't really Harvey."

She laughs. "That's fine. My name isn't really Emily. But it'll do under the circumstances."

"Fair enough," I smile. "Thanks, Emily."

"No problem, Harv." And she drives away.

I join Carly and Alan on the sidewalk. "See there, guys. No problem."

"Yeah, yeah," Carly says and kisses my cheek. "I really need to get going."

I grab her hands and say, "Call me tomorrow, okay?"

"Of course."

I glance back at Alan and then whisper into Carly's ear, "I'm just afraid, ya know, after he did this to me, of what he'll do to you."

"I'm only going to say this once," she says. "Do. Not. Worry. I can handle it."

She smiles and then runs off towards her house, leaving me and Alan to turn tail and do the same.

13

My eyes close and open and somehow hours have passed. Mom was asleep when I got home, so I let myself in, washed up, and crawled into bed. My face isn't too bad off. A few scrapes, light bruises, and a crushed nose. It'll heal. In the meantime, I'll blame the skate board. Those damn things are dangerous, or so I hear.

The sun is up and doing its best. It's streaming in through the window, past the slightly-opened shades.

Someone is tapping at my door. I look at my cell expecting it to be after noon at least, but to my surprise it's only 9:43. The tapping continues, so I drag myself up and stumble to the door in my boxers.

"Mom, it's early and it's Saturday. What gives?"

I open the door, but it isn't my mother. It's Carly. Stunning, beautiful, chorus-of-angels-singing-"Amazing Grace" Carly.

"Hi," she says. "Your mom said I should just come wake you up. I figured you'd still be asleep."

"Yeah, yeah. No problem. Come on in."

She steps inside and I shut the door behind her. She looks different. I notice she's not wearing any make-up, and I realize that I can't remember the last time I saw her without it.

"How'd your dad handle you coming home so late?" I ask.

"He had no clue. Still doesn't apparently. He was passed out when I got home, and hadn't moved a muscle when I left this morning."

"That's good," I say, honestly relieved, but only as a half-asleep person can be.

She unzips her coat and hangs it on the back of my computer chair. She's wearing a green cami over top of a long-sleeved black shirt. Her hair hangs just past her shoulders in haphazard pigtails that threaten innocence. She's gorgeous. Why in God's name did I never notice her before? Before... well, ya know. Before my little problem began.

"Shit, I'm in my underwear," I say, finally putting it all together. Yes, I'm in my underwear; no, it wasn't my mom at the door. It was Carly. The puzzle is complete, and damn it all, it reeks of embarrassment.

"Yes, you are," she laughs. "But that's okay. Nothing I haven't seen before, right?"

"Right," I say, but I feel my cheeks flushing red. Better my cheeks than my nose, I suppose.

I walk over to the bed and sit down, rubbing my eyes with the heels of my hands.

"What do you want to get into today?" I ask. "You sure this stuff with your dad will just blow over?"

She doesn't answer. Not at first. She just walks over and straddles me and kisses me hard – the kind of kiss where you can feel the pressure on your lips, teeth and tongue.

"I figured we could spend a couple hours in your room," she answers at last in between planting tiny kisses on my lips and neck.

She reaches down and pulls both of her shirts off and one red bra strap slips from her pale shoulder. I kiss her collar bone and then her neck. I want this so bad it hurts, but worry nags at the back of my mind. I can only imagine what her dad would do to her if he found out.

I look up at her and open my mouth – maybe to protest, maybe to say something strangely romantic – but she stops me with three fingers over my lips.

"Jace, don't talk. It's early. I'm tired and horny. You're hot. And this has been a long time coming."

We lie down on the bed and kiss for what seems like hours, over the course of which she slips free of her bra, pants and panties, and me of my boxers. We're all tangled up in each other, completely naked, and I have never wanted so desperately to live forever. We explore each other's bodies, first with our hands, and then our mouths, frantically seeking new textures, tastes and sensations.

She straddles me and I can feel her warmth hovering just above me. We're both breathing heavy, and I'm even shaking a little.

"Please tell me you have a condom," she says.

"Carly, please. I'm a 17-year-old male. Catching me without a condom would be like catching a preacher without a Bible."

***

I'm 17 and until then I was a virgin. Carly and I made love and it felt like forever. Not in the corny, "we'll be together for all time" sort of way, but in the sense that it would never end. Throughout, no worries entered my mind, and I would love to believe the same is true for her.

I always imagined my first time would be one of two ways: a). completely filthy, with a girl who knew far more than I did and had the sole purpose of "making a man out of me;" or b). awkward, fumbling and unfulfilling for anyone. It was clear that Carly was more experienced than me – I've known for quite some time that she wasn't a virgin – but it wasn't filthy and it damned sure wasn't unfulfilling. It was amazing.

She's sleeping on her stomach next to me and I take in every precious curve of her body. The first body I had ever experienced, and very well could be the last. Her skin would be a seamless pale cream color from her shoulders to the tips of her toes if not for the awful bruises on her back. They've healed some but still linger in various shades of green, blue and purple. Some may even be fresh. God, I hope not.

I place my hand on her left calf and drag it up her leg, over her ass and stop just short of the first bruise. Her skin is so soft, but cold. I hadn't even thought about the bruises while we were having sex. Had I carelessly pressed my fingers deep into her wounds while holding her? I have to push these things from my mind.

I lie down next to her and pull my blanket over both of us. I hold her until I, too, am fast asleep.

***

I wake up and it's still light outside, but just barely. Carly is still snoozing with the blanket pulled to just above her belly button and one hand above her head tangled in her hair. She looks like a picture – maybe a picture in a dirty mag, but a really classy one. I can't stop staring at her face, her body. In all my days as Carly's number one best friend, I never once saw her sexually. Never noticed how pretty – no, fuck it, beautiful – how beautiful she really is.

I don't really know how to process this. I want to kick her dad in the balls, wrap her in my arms, and let time make us wrinkly together.

I nudge her arm and she rolls onto her side but doesn't wake up. I slide my hand onto her stomach and pull her close to me. I kiss her, and awake or not, she kisses back.

"Hey, wake up. We've nearly wasted the whole day in bed."

"You call this wasting?" she says with sleep thick in her voice.

"Definitely not," I say and rub my hands up and down her back.

She's so amazing and this situation is so foreign and wonderful. I want my hands all over her at once.

"I just mean, my mom may start to talk. I don't want her to think I'm in here doing homework and becoming studious. She'd be so disappointed."

"Okay, okay. I just wish we could stay like this. You know?"

"Oh, I know. Forever, right?"

She smiles.

For the first time since I tasted Carly's lips, I remember that forever isn't real. Everybody dies. Some sooner than others.

We crawl out of bed and sluggishly – regretfully – pull on our clothes. We stroll out of the bedroom hand in hand and I expect my mom to at least shoot me a sideways glance as we walk by, but she isn't even home. I look in her bedroom, the living room, kitchen, and finally, in the driveway where I find her car is missing.

"Looks like you were worried for nothing," Carly says.

"How 'bout letting me walk you home?"

She glares at me from beneath a creased brow.

"How about halfway there?" she says. "Or even almost there. It may not be a good idea if my dad sees you just yet. You know, after what happened last night."

"Good point," I say. "Almost there it is."

We walk outside and responsible Jace is sure to lock the door behind him. I'm happy to turn around and see

Carly checking out Mal. Mal is sitting all sleek and sexy beneath a sinking sun. Her rust-red, partially pink paint job appears smooth and beautiful in the pale afternoon light. I suppose it's only natural for one sexy lady to attract another.

"When are you going to fix this thing up and get it on the road?" she says.

"Only a matter of time," I smirk. "Check this out."

I walk to the side of the car and work the door open, the hinges screeching – some would say in protest; I say they're cheering. I get inside, kick the trans into neutral, press the clutch and turn the key. Mal roars to life without a moment's hesitation.

"Sounds good," Carly says. "Go get your licenses already!" She kicks my thigh playfully.

"Can't. Not quite yet. Regardless of how good the ol' girl sounds, she won't pass the inspection. Her signal lights are sort of screwed up and the e-brake doesn't always hold the way it should. I'm about to get things in order though."

"Now, that's a damn shame. Think of how much fun we could have in this thing!"

"Are you kidding?" I say, turning to peer into the backseat. "Nothing but birth control seats back there. Contortionists could probably have some fun back there, but you and I may have a bit of trouble."

"Oh, shut up," she says. "We can have all of that type of fun we want… in your bedroom. Your mom obviously doesn't care. I just mean it would be cool to cruise this thing on the weekends. Get into all sorts of trouble."

"Yeah, I see your point. I'm working on it."

"Well, work faster." She smiles and grabs my ass.

"Easy," I say. "I'm tender."

Then I'm reminded of just how true those words really are.

***

I walk Carly home, skateboard in hand, stopping intermittently for her to take up the board and try her hand – or should I say feet – at boarding. After a few attempts, I let go of her waist and she rolls along, pushes off the ground a couple of times, but then fails at a sloppy ollie – which now that I think about it, sounds like urban slang for some extremely creative, yet poorly executed sex maneuver.

I kiss her goodbye a few blocks away so that we don't run into daddy-dearest, and watch her walk away until she is out of sight. I return home on foot dangling the board at my side, trying not to think that Carly is walking into a shit-storm of drunken fists, belts and God knows what else.

It's an odd mind state, mixed with worry and extreme happiness. On one hand, it's official: I will not die a virgin. I could die this second, and still not die a virgin. But knowing Carly's problem, I can't give in to happiness. A part of me wants to rush back to her house and protect her. Another part knows that's a terrible idea. Her dad would kick my ass right along with hers. If we can just hold out a few more weeks, Carly will be 18 and can get out of that house forever.

I wonder how long this shit has been going on. I can remember her showing up to school with a busted lip, once a black eye. But she always had a handy excuse to write it off to nothing. I never thought anything more of it, and it kills me that I didn't.

Mom's car is in the driveway when my house comes into view. I leave the skateboard on the porch and come in through the front door.

"Hey stud," she says. "When did your little friend leave?"

"A few hours ago," I say nonchalantly as I make my way to the kitchen and open the fridge.

Mom persists.

"You all sure were in there for a long time."

I can see her sly smile from the kitchen. Taunting your son about sex, what kind of mother are you? The coolest, I suppose.

"Yeah, we were playing Scrabble. You'd be proud. I won." I pull some cold cuts, cheese and mayo out of the fridge, and place them on the counter next to a half loaf of wheat bread.

"Oh, is that what you kids are calling it these days? That's fine. But remember, there are no winners. Scrabble should be mutually beneficial for all parties."

"You were a whore in high school weren't you? I knew it!"

"Takes one to know one, kiddo."

I roll my eyes and put the hat on my sandwich, then place the cold goods back in the fridge.

"I'll be in my love den if you need me," I say, and then retreat to my room and close the door. Man, Mom can be brutal when she puts her mind to it.

14

It's not long before I'm fast asleep, dreaming my teenage dreams. I wake up to a small sound, a tapping. I'm not sure it is real when I first open my eyes. I glance around the room and see light from the street lamps struggling to get through the blinds. My sandwich plate is still sitting on the desk, dusted with crumbs and a single smear of mayonnaise.

But the tapping persists.

I sit up and creep over to the window and part the blinds a little further. Carly is standing outside. My heart skips a few beats. My pulse quickens. I panic. I raise the blinds and open the window and she crawls inside. That brief instant that the window is open reminds me how cold it is outside. The harsh night air bites my naked chest before I pull the window shut.

Carly is sobbing.

I can see that her face is discolored even with the light off. That son of a bitch!

She buries her head in my chest and sobs, dropping her school bag to the floor. She's wearing jeans and a Billy Idol t-shirt. She's not even wearing a coat. I place my arms around her and hug her close. It feels like hugging an ice sculpture.

"You're okay," I say.

I reach towards the desk and flip on the lamp. When she looks up I see just how bad it really is. Her face is discolored, an odd shade of red and blue. Her lip is swollen badly and crusted with dried blood that trails around the curve of her chin. Dried blood is also crusted around her noise and her left eye is nearly swollen shut.

"It's never been this bad," she says.

I can't speak. I don't know what to say or do. I just look at her, horrified.

"It's never been this bad!" she repeats through hoarse coughs and gasps.

I run my hand through her hair, brushing the tear-matted strands back off her face.

"Let's get you cleaned up," I finally manage.

I help her to the bathroom quietly, taking care not to wake Mom. She turns the cold water on and dips her head down into the sink, splashing her face and rubbing it gently. I'm shaking as I watch, holding a towel for her to pat her wounds dry.

Normally, it's me with the bloody face in the sink. And that's the way I like it. Uh huh. Uh huh. Not Carly.

She rises up and takes the towel and holds it over her face. I shudder at the thought of her going head to head with her dad while I'm snoozing away. Kids deserve the right to go to bed, damn it. And ultimately, we're kids. I have no delusions about that, unlike a lot of the people at school. I'm a kid, even though just barely.

We walk back to my room and I shut and lock the door. I would love to say that her face looks much better after a quick cleansing, but I'd be lying.

"We'll just chill here until morning, then we'll tell my mom what's going on," I say.

"I don't know," she says. Her sobs have subsided, but she still has a shudder in her voice. "My dad is probably out looking for me right now. He may not know where you live, but he'll probably find out pretty soon. We need to get out of here."

"Let's go. We can leave tonight, crash somewhere, then come back and get my mom on board in the morning."

"I just don't know what to do," she says. "I don't want to tell anyone. I just want to get out of here. Get out of here and never come back."

I want to tell her that's impossible, but I can't. Deep down she has to know that isn't a realistic option. I just can't tell her no.

"Okay, let's go."

She looks at me, mouth gaping, like I just suggested we both quit school and become jewel thieves.

"Are you serious? Where will we go?"

"That doesn't matter right now. I just know that we can't be here when your dad gets here. We'll figure out the details on the way."

"He'll find us. He'll catch us." Her voice is shaking and her hands are trembling.

"Not if we take Mal."

I fully expected, for reasons unknown, the full motherly speech about responsibility, not having a license, the consequences of getting caught, and so on, but all Carly says is, "Okay."

"Give me five minutes to get ready."

I quickly toss on a faded red t-shirt, some jeans, socks and shoes. I put some extra clothes in my book bag, grab a coat for Carly and one for myself. She puts it on, an extra thick *Emerica* hoodie, red with maroon stripes. It engulfs her tiny frame.

I open the bottom drawer of my desk and retrieve an old stained envelope. Inside is all the money I'd been saving to put the finishing touches on Mal. I take out the money and count it: $187. After some quick math regarding current gas prices, I thank my lucky stars that Mal is only a 6 cylinder.

There's no sense in creeping through the house and taking the chance of waking up mom, so after cramming some extra clothes into my bag, I snag my keys and Carly and I climb out my window. I turn and ease the window back down. We dash across the lawn to where Mal is parked. Luckily, she's completely put together on this particular night. Sometimes I feel adventurous and go poking and prodding, tinkering with the machine, but not on this particular day.

I unlock the driver's side door and ease it open. Mal tends to protest in a noisy way if you open the door too fast. I throw my bag into the back seat, get inside and ease the door shut, reach across and unlock Carly's door. She climbs inside and places her bag at her feet.

It's silent in the car. I put the keys in the ignition and am about to crank the engine to life when something occurs to me: I should leave a note for Mom. Not tell her exactly where I'm going – partially because I don't know – but give her an idea that I'm alright and not to freak out.

"I'll be right back," I say.

I get out of the car and scamper back across the lawn, pry open my bedroom window and climb inside. I grab a sheet of paper and quickly scrawl a note:

Mom,
If I've ever needed you to trust me, it's now. I'm okay. Be back in a few days. Something came up. Trust me.

I place the note on the closed toilet lid – where I'm sure she'll find it – and head back to the car. Carly is asleep in the passenger's seat when I return. I see no need to wake her up. I start the car, wincing at the initial roar of the engine, then back her out onto the street. I'm very light on the gas until my house is well behind us, then I open her up a little, though still careful to mind the speed limit.

I glance at Carly and she seems peaceful. We're off, I suppose. I just wish I knew where we're going.

***

My mind is racing with all sort of terrible thoughts. It won't be long – if not already – before Carly's dad puts two and two together, starts looking for us and most likely notifies the police. The pale orange glow of the dashboard gauges, which normally feels soothing, now feels like "caution" or "warning" lights, which I suppose makes much more sense.

I get out of the downtown area quickly and onto the Interstate where traffic is more frequent and we're not the sole vehicle cruising the suburban streets at 3 in the morning.

I push Mal on up to 70 mph and hold it steady. Every car I see approaching in the rear view mirror suddenly seems threatening. I keep expecting blue lights, followed by a trip down town, while Carly is returned home to her dad. That cannot happen.

I quickly scan my brain for a place to park the car overnight where we won't be found. Being on the road isn't a good idea, economically or logically. All I need is somewhere away from towns where the car won't be seen. Maybe Jones' Mill Road, where suburban America gives way to farmland and eventually blacktop gives way to gravel.

I take the exit and make a right at the end of the ramp. Jones' Mill Road is dead ahead.

Southland Drive, the road that will eventually become Jones' Mill, is four lanes and lined with restaurants and shopping centers on both sides. Occasionally, I see a small apartment complex. The four lanes eventually become two and all signs of businesses and night-life stop. There are empty fields and farm houses, barns and pastures. It's like I just drove through a teleportation device to another time.

There are hardly any lights on at all, a very good sign – only the occasional porch light or street light. The only sound is the steady hum of Mal's engine, pushing the car along at 30 mph or so.

I see a dirt road up ahead to the right that leads down between two fields. Man, I wish it were fall or late summer. Then there would probably be towering corn stalks on each side. I turn onto it and hope for the best.

Jostling down the path, I see a barn in the distance, wearing worn red paint. I back in behind the barn, putting the back bumper as close as possible to an old tractor parked there. I get out and double check that the nose of the car isn't sticking out, practically screaming, "Hello world, I'm a fugitive. Please arrest me!" The ground crunches beneath my feet like I'm walking on brittle bones.

Behind the tractor is an old Caprice, sitting on two flat tires. Its windshield is frosted over, just like every other stationary object on this cold February night.

Once back inside the car – when I close the car door, it sounds like thunder in the otherwise silent field – I try to relax while absolutely terrible thoughts race through my head. I imagine trying to leave this tiny dirt lane and meeting a full scale police road block at the end. The bloody ends of several movies run through my head and I shudder.

How many decisions were just made without thinking? I don't even want to try to count them. I tilt the driver's seat back as far as it will go, zip my jacket and settle back with my arms crossed across my chest. Carly is still sleeping, her head pressed against the window, which I can only imagine is bitter cold and uncomfortable. I reach into the backseat and take a couple of crumpled shirts out of my bag. I lift her head off the freezing window and place the shirts underneath.

There. Now. Sleepy time.

15

I wake to a terrible noise the next morning. It's my phone. Not the wrath of God, and more importantly, not Carly's father.

I free it from my jeans pocket and the tiny screen informs me that "Alan is calling…"

"Hello," I say, holding the freezing phone to my cheek.

The light outside is blinding, the sun out in full force. It shines through the frost-caked windshield, which only amplifies its brightness.

"Jace, where the hell are you, man?"

Ah, Alan. The ever-present voice of reason. Where the hell were you last night?

"Currently, I'm hiding from a crazed psychopath and most likely the police – who have somehow teamed up – behind an old barn. How's your morning going?"

"Well, I'm at home, wondering where my two best friends are. Your mom called, said Carly's dad was looking for her. She's with you, isn't she?" Alan sounds frantic. I can hear the quiver in his voice, and can only imagine his entire body is shaking along with it.

"Why, yes she is. Would you like to say hi?"

"Dude. Stop joking around. This is serious. Everybody is looking for you! You could be in some serious shit, man. Her dad was talking about kidnapping charges."

"Oh, that's fucking stupid. How does the old saying go? 'You can't kidnap the willing.'"

"I'm not well-versed enough in the law to tell you either way. I just want to know what's going on. This isn't very characteristic of you or Carly."

"Her dad, man. He beat the shit out of her last night. She showed up at my house at like 2 in the morning. How could I let her go back home to that?" Now my voice is quivering.

"Seriously? Are you messing with me?" he says.

"No. It's been going on for a while. She just didn't know how to tell you. I'm sorry for keeping you in the dark, man."

"Holy shit! Is she okay?" Alan shouts.

"She's a little beat up, but she's okay."

Alan is silent for a moment. I expect he's weighing how to most delicately call me a short-sighted asshole.

"I understand what you're trying to do," he says. "But there has to be a better option. Can't you go to the police?"

"I thought about that," I say. "I figure there's nothing they can do immediately. It would probably go one of two ways: Carly goes home while police investigate, and her dad could possibly kill her, at the very least beat her half to death in the meantime; or the police take her away from her dad and she spends some time God only knows where. She doesn't have a mom, you know."

"Yeah, but she's going to be 18 in like two weeks or something. She can spend a little time in foster care. It's better than the alternative."

"But we can't guarantee that's what will happen! And damn it all, I can't take that chance."

I notice Carly is awake now, sitting up straight in the passenger's seat and staring at me wide-eyed.

"Who is that?" she mouths silently.

"Alan," I reply. She relaxes a bit and slumps back into the seat.

"I get that, I suppose," Alan says. "So, what's your plan?"

"It happened pretty fast," I say. "I guess we don't really have one."

"That is so you. Doing and then thinking."

"Hey man, why don't you can that shit! If you have nothing constructive to add to this situation, I'm out."

"Cool it," Alan says. "I'm happy to help in any way that I can. But I feel I need to be critical here. You're not being critical, so someone has to be."

"Yeah, I guess you're right. My head is way up in the clouds here."

"Besides, we've been friends a long time. It's not our style to be divided like this."

"Agreed," I say. "So, what do ya got?"

Carly is looking out the window into the frosted field. I wonder if she's paying attention to anything I say.

"First of all, information is power. I'll keep my ears open for anything and get that information to you. But I won't call your cell. You're going to turn it off and leave it off. They can trace it."

"Shit. I hadn't thought of that."

"Yeah, so when we hang up, turn it off. Call me from pay phones. We'll determine a time for the next call each time we hang up. I don't know how long we can keep this up, but…"

"Wait a minute," I say, momentarily suffering from a stroke of genius. "We only have to keep this up for 12 days tops."

"Come again."

"Carly will be 18 in 12 days, and then she won't have to go home."

I see her perk up at the sound of her name. She turns away from the window and is staring at me with wide eyes. Seeing her face, battered and bruised, in the breaking day light destroys me. I can't stand it. I turn my attention back to the phone and stare at my lap, only now realizing just how cold I am.

"Yeah, man. That makes sense. If you can pull this off, you'd be saving her ass. And probably saving your own ass by staying out of jail. Though, again, I'm not a master of the law, so I can't say anything for sure."

"I'm not even worried about what happens to me. I know my mom will let her stay at our house if she knows what's going on. I just want to make sure she's safe. Nobody deserves what that dick has been doing to her."

I'm very aware of Carly's presence as these words leave my mouth.

"Dear, noble Jace. Our knight in shining armor," Alan mocks.

"Oh shut up, man," I laugh.

"Well, at least this resembles a plan. I feel better about this."

"Yeah, sounds good," I say. "Just do me one favor before we talk next time. Call my mom back. Make sure she's okay. Don't tell her anything. Just make sure she got my note and she's on board."

Alan considers this a moment. I know he doesn't like being deceptive.

"Okay," he says. "I can do that."

"Thanks, man. I'll call you around midnight. I think we'll just hang out here and pray that no one finds us, and then head out on the Interstate after dark."

"That sounds like a plan," Alan says. "Let me know if there is anything I can do to help."

"Sure thing. Catch you later."

I hang up the phone and immediately turn it off as Alan had suggested. I turn to Carly.

"How much of that did you hear?" I ask.

"Enough to get a general idea," she says. "So, we're going on the run until I'm 18? Is that the plan?"

"More or less," I say. "But it sounds so much more illegal when you put it that way."

She laughs. "You're really sticking your neck out for me here. Thanks."

"It's no problem at all," I say. "You took my virginity. It's the least I can do."

"What the fuck?" she laughs. "How do you manage to pull off being a complete asshole, yet strangely romantic at the same time?"

"Pure talent," I say. "Something I was born with."

"Apparently. So, what's next?"

Her breath steams out of her mouth along with her words, creating a momentary white cloud in front of her face.

"We just chill," I say, hugging my jacket a little tighter around my shivering body. "No pun intended."

16

The day passes slowly. Carly and I discuss growing up, and she occasionally drops in something like, "Oh yeah, remember that time I fell off the swings and broke my arm? That was a lie. My dad broke it pulling me up off the floor." She speaks as if a huge weight has been lifted from her. I am happy to listen, even though it isn't the happiest of topics.

We also discuss the twelve days to come. We determine we'll lay low during the day time, and drive after dark, trying to put as much physical space between us and Hemingford as possible. By noon the sun has melted the frost off the windshield completely and we can see just how far these fields stretch. There are houses in the distance, but they're so far away we're not worried about them noticing us.

The sky is blue and the sun is deceivingly bright, though it is much warmer than it was a few hours ago. We keep our jackets pulled tight and try to keep our minds off the cold, and worse, being caught. We're both hungry but there's nothing to eat. Eating will definitely be a priority once we get a few miles under the ol' belt.

Around 4:45, as the sun is on its way down, though not quite there yet, dark clouds fill the sky. It's nearly 5 when the first flurries start to fall. Damn it. Anyone who knows anything about cars would know that the least amount of precipitation can mean certain doom for a rear-wheel-drive vehicle – a.k.a. nearly every sports car ever put together.

I must admit, modestly, that my driving skills are beyond that of your standard 17-year-old who doesn't have a license. However, my practice time in snow has been very limited. This entire venture has been one big hoping-for-the-best situation. We can only hope that flurries are as bad as it gets. But each tiny flake that flecks the windshield makes my heart sink a little lower.

Once it's dark, I ease Mal out of our temporary parking spot. Thankfully, the frosted ground crunches beneath her tires instead of slipping and allowing the tires to spin. I ease out to the end of the lane where I see two lanes of snow-dusted blacktop.

"Something wrong?" Carly asks, after we sit still for a moment, me just looking at the road.

"Camaros aren't the best cars to drive in snow," I say.

"It's just a little snow," she says with a smirk.

"A little snow to a Camaro is like a raging blizzard to the average car." I try to put on a smile, but it's drenched in worry.

"I trust you," Carly says.

I make sure the shifter is in first gear, give the gas pedal a few light taps and ease off the clutch. Again, the car doesn't spin, but rolls over the crunchy, frosted ground. Once on the asphalt, every muscle in my body tenses and I expect the car to lose control and turn circles in the middle of the road at any minute. Every time I change gears, I hold my breath.

I don't dare attempt the speed limit, which is currently a deadly 45 miles per hour. I keep it at a steady 35 just to be on the safe side, and every time a car passes in the opposite lane, a gust of frigid wind shakes the car just slightly. Whoever they are, they're going much faster than us. Crazy kids!

The two-lane road eventually turns to four and the speed limit jumps to 55. I figure I can press on a little faster so we don't stand out as the one car doing 20 miles under the legal speed, but I won't try more than 40. The snow is coming down harder now and the road appears to be solid white in the glow of my headlights.

The exit for the Interstate is coming up, so I slow down and prepare to make the right-hand turn. I swear I can feel the back tires shift as I begin the turn. I clutch the steering wheel with both hands, completely forgetting to downshift. The engine sputters and I press the clutch and fumble with the shifter, eventually getting it to stick in second gear. When I let off the clutch again, I give a little too much gas and the back tires spin and the car swings out to the left. Carly gasps and clutches the door handle and the side of her seat.

For a second, I expect the rear bumper to crash into the guardrail. I brace for the sudden jolt, but thankfully it never comes. The tires seem to have caught some traction, so I ease into third gear and slowly drive down the exit ramp.

Once on the Interstate, a gale of other vehicles rushes by and Mal jostles. We're trucking along at a steady 40 miles per hour. The other traffic seems to barely notice it's snowing, some of them probably pushing 80.

We drive on slowly for close to an hour without saying a word. At this point I realize I haven't spared Carly's father or the police a single thought. I've been too concerned with other things, I suppose.

"I'm going to try to go a little faster," I say, fears of blue lights finally coming into play.

"Just be careful," Carly urges.

I push the car up to 60, still a little slow given the 70 mph speed limit. Cars continue to rush by, but none of them seem to pay any attention to us. The lonely Camaro struggling to make its way down a treacherous road – the little Camaro that could. How poetic.

"I figure we need to get pretty far from Hemingford before we stop for gas," I say. "People are probably looking for us all over back home. Let's hope we haven't made the news."

"You think we'll make the news?"

"The way Alan was talking, I would almost guarantee it."

"Ha," Carly says. "Famous at last."

"Yeah, if this was a crime drama, you would be the helpless victim," I say. "At least in the eyes of the media. And I'm the violent, socially misunderstood kidnapper."

"But that's not true at all. Surely everyone will realize that once all this is over."

"I hope so."

We had been traveling for close to five hours when the gas hand suggests we pull off for a refill. I see an exit sign that boasts a gaggle of gas stations, so I hit the blinker and begin to slow down. At the end of the exit ramp, a tiny two-lane road awaits, sparkling with fresh snow. I ease out onto the road and make an almost immediate right into the parking lot of the first gas station I see.

It's dark in the car, the overhead lights of the gas station casting harsh shadows across Carly's face.

"I'm going to run inside and grab some food. It won't be *Healthy Choice,* but at least it'll shut our stomachs up."

"You think it's okay to go in? I mean, what if they recognize you?"

"It's chance it or starve to death, I suppose. Not to mention we don't have the luxury of paying at the pump." I unzip my bag and pull out a wad of folded bills. "Just sit tight. I'll be careful and I'll be quick."

I close the door and look around. I feel naked out in the open like this with cars buzzing about and people gassing their vehicles and coming to and from the front door of the gas station.

I'd like to note that this is nothing like Sugarman's station. Sugarman's is a true service station. He'll fix your car, pump up your tires, change your wiper blades. Hell, he'd even pump your gas for you at no extra charge. This place is your standard, run-of-the-mill super gas station chain. No charm. No personality. Just corporate America at its finest. *Super America!*

I walk inside with a confident stride. I've always been a class-A bullshitter, so I put on my best bullshit, happy-go-lucky expression. There's nothing wrong folks! I'm just your average, cliché American teenager, looking to illegally buy some smokes, drive too fast and fuck random girls without condoms.

If that's the worst people think of me, oddly enough, I should be fine.

There's a few people here and there, browsing beverages, picking through snacks. A couple of men dressed in heavy winter garb just stand by sipping coffee and talking while leaning on the far end of the counter.

I walk back to the snack section and grab a fistful of *Nutri-Grain* bars, a couple bags of chips, a few bags of peanuts – super cheap, 2 for $1! – and a 24 pack of *Pepsi*. I walk up to the counter and put down my armload of snacks, hopefully enough to last us a week if we snack sparingly, and wait for the attention of the cashier.

The cashier is a portly young woman whose nametag reads "Beth." She's leaning against the back counter frantically thumbing her cellphone, trying to squeeze in that last text message before returning to her duties.

Lucky for me, when she finally begins ringing up my items she doesn't lift her eyes. Completely detached. Thank God.

"I also need $30 in gas on pump 7, please," I say, looking out the window at Mal and Carly. Carly is shifting her weight in the seat and glancing from side to side. Not conspicuous at all, baby. Please, please, please calm down.

"$57.81," Beth says.

The hairs on the back of my neck stand up when she addresses me and the feeling of nakedness washes over me again. I plunge my right hand into my jeans pocket and pull out the wad of money. I hand her $60 in assorted bills – George, Abraham, Andrew, the gang's all here. She takes it, punches the cash register with a chubby finger, then hands me back my change.

There are people standing behind me now. Just their presence makes me uneasy, but I dare not turn around to sneak a glance at them. It could be a cop. Or worse, but not likely, it could be Carly's dad. I chuckle at the thought. Now I'm just being ridiculous.

"Something funny?" Beth asks while putting the last of my snacks into a flimsy plastic bag.

"Hmm? Oh, no. Just thinking about something I heard yesterday. Sorry."

"Did you know your nose is bleeding?"

"Say what?" I instinctively raise my hand to my nose and sure enough I feel a crusty dried mess. "Ah shit! It's this cold weather, ya know? It does this to me every year. Excuse me."

I grab the bag of snacks and head for the men's room. Not now! Worst possible timing. It's strange. I haven't worried about my leaky honker since we left my house last night. It's still a pressing matter, of course. If I die while Carly and I are on this little venture, it surely will not bode well for our cause.

I look into the mirror and thankfully it's not bad. It's not currently bleeding, but it had been. There's a ring of dried blood around my right nostril and trailing down towards the curve of my upper lip. You can barely notice it.

I turn on the cold water and splash some onto my face. A couple of cheap paper towels should do the trick. I barely moisten one and rub at the crusty blood. In a matter of seconds, it's gone and I'm heading back through the station and towards the car.

It's gotten colder. I pump the gas as quickly as the pump will allow, hugging myself tightly as the super corporate gas pump ticks along slowly. It gets just above $29 and the tiny digital numbers slow to a crawl. Why the fuck do they do that? There's no reason for it that I can see, other than to make perfectly good citizens, and in this case fugitives, stand and watch while freezing their balls off.

Of course, $30 doesn't fill Mal up, but it's close. This should get us a pretty good distance, where it should be okay to stop again for gas. Of course, we'll have to stop somewhere before that to call Alan. But honestly, these days I don't even know where to look for a payphone like they have in old movies and TV shows, and it's way too dangerous to walk into a place of business and ask to use theirs.

We'll figure something out. It's only a little after 10:30, so we still have time.

I settle into the driver's seat and put the bag of snacks in the back. Carly is sitting up straight with the sun visor pulled down, carefully applying lipstick, having already applied eye shadow. Strangely enough, she now looks more like the Carly I've spent my childhood with.

"Much better," she says, giving herself an approving look in the mirror. She places the tube of lipstick back into her bag and puts it into the backseat along with everything else we currently own.

I can smell her lipstick from where I sit. It's a pearlescent plum color, but reeks of black licorice. She reaches across the console and kisses my lips. The kiss is wonderful, but as she pulls away, the taste of black licorice – cursed Sweet Annie – lingers.

Suddenly, I'm five years old again, looking at Aunt Dolly's body lying in a casket and knowing that someday I will be in the same place – dead in a coffin. Possibly sooner rather than later.

17

In all her 1980's glory, Mal's dashboard display informs me that it's pushing midnight when we cross the Tennessee state line. The roads have been mostly clear and traffic has been sparse.

Alan is probably going out of his mind with worry, thinking we've been caught or maybe even lying on the side of the road dead. Alan is such a worrier. Sort of like the chubby, underage father I never had. Regardless, it isn't worth the risk to confidently stroll into a gas station, convenience store or even a Wal-Mart to use a phone. Maybe we can chance it now that we are in Tennessee. Surely news has some boarders, at least in its infancy.

Carly and I haven't spoken in at least an hour. She is sitting with her seat leaning way back, possibly asleep. I break the silence anyway. My worried mind can't take the silence much more.

"We need to call Alan," I say. "Any ideas?"

"How much money do we have left?" she says.

"Not as much as we need. Why?"

"I was thinking that maybe we could buy one of those pay-as-you-go phones. It would really come in handy."

"Yeah, I'm not exactly sure how much one of those things cost, but it's probably more than we can afford. Got anything else?"

"How important is it that we even call Alan?" she says. "Rate it. Scale of one to ten."

"Probably about an eight, to be honest. Aside from the fact that he's probably worrying himself into a receding hairline and a possible nervous breakdown, we should at least find out what people are saying or if we've made the news yet."

"I guess you're right. Then let's just stop somewhere. It worked back at the gas station. It could work again."

"I would really hate to be wrong. I would be in jail by morning and you'd be back with your dad."

"Try to be a little more positive," she says through what is clearly a forced smile.

I force a smile back.

"Just run it one more time through that brilliant little brain of yours. Please! We need a place that is somewhat secluded, non-traceable and where we would have very little contact with other people."

"What about a rest area? Those places would probably still have payphones."

I glance at her, perhaps a little slack-jawed.

"Holy shit. Why didn't I think of that? Like I said, you're brilliant! I could kiss you!"

"What's stopping you?" she says.

"As amazing as you are, I dare not take my eyes off this road. I'm almost positive we would die."

"Good reason. I'll just bank the kiss for when we stop."

***

Within 20 minutes, a giant green sign reads, "Rest Area – Next Exit." As soon as the car stops, Carly kisses me hard, and as glorious as it is, that God-awful lip stick comes hellishly close to ruining it. I can't help but shudder at the aftertaste once our lips part.

"I'll check it out and see if there's a payphone."

"I'm coming with you. I need to stretch my legs. I've been in this car far too long. No offense, Mal," she quickly adds, giving a sympathetic pat to the dashboard.

"I'm not sure that's a great idea. We're probably about 1000 times more recognizable together."

"Jace, fuck off. I'm getting out of this car. Look around! There's no one here! It'll be fine."

I cast a nervous glance around the parking lot, seeking anything that could even possibly be another human being. It's deserted, like Carly said, and the overhead lights cast a pale, forgotten glow on the cracked pavement and dilapidated wooden shacks that housed restrooms, snack machines and hopefully payphones.

"Okay. I'm sorry. Let's just make it quick."

We get out simultaneously and I wince when Carly's door closes. I ease mine shut in a paranoid sort of way. The air outside possesses an unpleasant bite, the complete opposite of what we've been used to inside Mal. Say what you want to about the old girl, but don't knock the heater.

There is about an inch of snow that crunches beneath our feet, though the snow has stopped for the moment. The two buildings, a "His" and "Hers," connected by a rickety awning await us at the end of a slender, concrete walkway. The concrete is cracked – the perfect place for weeds to sprout up in the spring. It is a pale orange in the light of the overheads.

Just when we are about to go separate ways to search for a payphone, I see two of them resting beneath the awning. They're boxy old things, with worn blue sides, color missing altogether in some places.

"There," I say. I point. We walk.

I dig into my pocket and fish out a handful of change. I shove two quarters into the machine and quickly dial Alan's number. The phone rings once, twice. I glance over my shoulder to ensure that the parking lot is still deserted.

"Hello!" Alan says after the third ring, not even trying to conceal his anxiety. High strung Alan, just as expected.

"Hey. Guess who?"

"Jace? Thank God. Are you two okay? I've been worried shitless!"

"Come up for air, bro. We're fine. We just had a bit of a problem finding a phone."

"Where are you?" he says.

"We're at a rest stop about 15 minutes across the Tennessee state line," I say. "On a pay phone. How cool is that?"

"Dude, be serious."

"Okay, sorry. So, what's the good word on your two favorite fugitives?"

"It's not good. They have issued an Amber Alert, meaning pretty much every cop and good Samaritan in the state is looking for you."

"Lucky for us, we're not in Kansas, err… Kentucky anymore."

"You won't be safe for long," Alan says. "You two need to get off the road and lay low for a while. This is really serious. You could go to prison."

"Relax, buddy. Only 11 more days to go. We'll figure it out."

I have always felt the urge to play it cool with Alan. I feel that if I stumble, even slightly, he will crumble. And I just can't do that to the poor guy.

"Yeah, just play it safe. Take zero chances. Please."

"You got it," I say as sincerely as I can muster.

"By the way, they…"

"Oh shit!" Carly says. "Jace, look! Someone's here."

I look at the parking lot and see a dark hatchback sitting next to Mal.

"Oh fuck. How long has that car been there?" I say.

"Not sure," Carly says. "I just looked up and saw it."

"Did they see us?"

"Probably not. I had to peek around the corner to see the car. But we need to get the hell out of here."

She's starting to panic, and rightfully so.

"Alan, I have to go. We got company."

Before he says a word, I slam the receiver down and take Carly by the hand.

"In here," I say, and we step into the men's room.

It's dingy, as expected, and one overhead light is flickering wildly in the corner, creating an eerie strobe effect. There is a row of windows high above the sinks – blurred glass, so no one can see your naughty bits.

"Get down," I say, and then I climb upon the sink and peer out. "It looks like a woman. Dressed nice. She's poking around out there, looking in the car windows and such."

I'm squinting hard to peer through the blurred glass and can just barely make her out in the distance.

"Do you think she's a cop?"

"Could be. Maybe a detective. It looks like she's wearing a pants suit. So, I guess the dress code fits."

"Oh shit! Shit! What are we going to do?" Carly says.

"Calm down," I say, glancing over my shoulder from atop the sink. "Maybe she'll go in the ladies room to freshen up and we can sneak away undetected."

"If she's poking around in your car, I don't think she's here to freshen up," Carly says. She's now backed herself into a stall and is sitting on a toilet lid. She looks like a small child, frightened to death by that one dreaded fear about to become a reality. I feel the same fear, but I dare not let it show.

The lady is now walking down the slender concrete path towards the shacks. Towards Carly and I.

"Oh shit," I say. "We need to get out of here."

The lady steps out of view. Lucky for us, the payphones and the doors to the bathrooms are on the opposite side of the tiny shack than where the windows are. I push hard on one of the windows, but it doesn't budge. I think I am officially panicking. I ram my shoulder into the window as hard as I can, but it doesn't open. Instead, the glass cracks along the middle and comes out in two solid rectangular chunks.

I motion to Carly. "Come on!"

She scrambles up on to the sink and I help her out the window, and then quickly follow. It's a tiny opening and difficult to squeeze through, despite us both being a little on the scrawny side.

When I get to my feet, the woman is nowhere in sight. Thankfully!

"Come on," I whisper. "Let's get the hell out of here!"

We sneak across the frosted grass, around the side of the shack and down the walkway. Hell, maybe she did go to freshen up. Because I don't see her anywhere. Carly and I get into Mal quickly and slam the doors a little harder than we should have. I fumble the key into the ignition and turn. Nothing happens. Of course! Of all the unbelievable times for this car to fuck up. I turn again. Nothing.

Carly looks at me in disbelief.

"Hold up. I can fix this," I say, pulling the hood release and bolting out of the car.

I lift the hood and remember how I always fixed this before, which was purely by luck. I truly have no idea why this happens. But it does. Sometimes the ol' girl just doesn't feel like running.

Don't panic, Jace. Fiddling with wires and terminals always worked before, so fiddle like you've never fiddled before. The image of me haphazardly attempting to play an actual fiddle sprinted across my mind, but vanished quickly, before I even had time to chuckle at it.

I grab a nearby rock and tap at the battery terminals, which seem to be attached just fine. I grab hold of the wiring leading to the terminals and shimmy them back and forth. I cuss at the car under my breath. Okay. That's all the old tricks.

I hurry back into the vehicle and close the door. I take a deep breath before trying the engine again. This time, she cranks, turns over and roars to life.

Curse the sound of your engine, Malory Guile! It swells into the otherwise silent night, like a boisterous fart in church. I back out and head for the roadway, while Carly cranes her neck to peer behind us.

"See her anywhere?" I say.

"Oh shit! She just ran out of the lady's room! And she's running after us."

"Unless she's the *T-1000* I think we're good. She can't catch us on foot."

I'm almost positive I heard the lady scream my name, though only faintly.

I breathe a heavy sigh of relief. Was I holding my breath that whole time? I don't think so, but it sure feels like it.

"For once, I think Alan is right. We need to get this thing off the road and lay low for a while." I say.

"For once?"

"Okay, okay. As usual."

18

We're not on the road again more than 15 minutes before snow starts to fly. It's much worse this time. I can barely see. I remember when I was little, always a passenger, seeing snow flying into Mom's oncoming headlights and thinking, "this is just like space travel, like in the *Star Wars* movies." It was mysterious and wonderful. Now, not so much.

"Now would be an awesome time to find a place to pull over," Carly says.

She's biting her lip and I can tell she's scared. I know the feeling.

"Any ideas? I'm not exactly sure where we are."

"Me either."

I squint through the oncoming asteroids and only see about five feet of asphalt in front of the car. I see no oncoming headlights. Are we really the only ones dumb enough to be out – though in our defense, we were sort of forced into this.

"I think I see an exit up ahead. I think we should take it," Carly says.

"What if it goes into a city or something, lots of people plus fugitives usually equals caught fugitives."

"Please give that shit a rest. We're not fugitives!"

"Yeah, everyone just thinks we are."

"Caught is better than dead, though. Just take it!"

"Okay, but remember, it was your idea."

I click the right blinker and slow down to take the exit ramp. It's a short straight ramp and we skid to a halt at the end, where I am relieved to see a tiny two-lane road and no traffic. I ease off the clutch and attempt to turn right.

The back tires start to spin on the slick ground and the car begins to slide towards the guard rail. I panic! I let off the gas and stomp the break but it's too late. The back bumper connects with the guardrail with a jolt.

"Shit!"

Again, I ease off the clutch and give it considerably less gas. Mal struggles to pull out, but slides sporadically. Eventually, the tires catch enough traction and we ease onto the road.

"Oh my God, Jace. Please be careful!"

My heart is pounding so fast I can feel it in my throat.

"We need to find a place to pull over, but not just any place will do. We need to find a place to hide!" I say.

"Just pull over somewhere," Carly says. "We can park and if the snow keeps coming, it will cover our tracks and maybe even the car."

Genius! The way it's snowing, it will almost surely cover everything in a couple of hours, if not less. I begin looking for a place to turn off the main road, but as I scan the roadsides, a curve comes into view and I turn the wheel much too fast. The car loses all traction and the rear tires swing wide. I fight it by cutting the wheel in the opposite direction, but it's too late. Mal slides off the road and the passenger door connects with a large tree.

The seatbelt grips my shoulder and waist, holding me firmly to the seat. I look at Carly and she seems okay, but she looks back at me with wide, frightened eyes. The car creaks, moans and begins to slide again. It's now that I realize the tree actually did us a favor by stopping us from going down a large embankment. But the favor was only a temporary one. The car is still sliding. I think briefly about grabbing Carly and jumping out, but that would never work.

We both scream.

I reach across and hold her tightly as Mal slides head first down the snowy bank and into the black unknown.

***

I'm not sure how long we were unconscious, or how far the car rolled before it crashed at the bottom. I'm pretty sure it was a tree that ended our little joyride, but I can't be sure. The last thing I remember was the rush of snow coming towards us, then sharp pain, and then blackness.

"Carly?" I whimper. "Carly?"

No answer. I turn to my right, expecting the worst, to see Carly unconscious or even dead. Instead, she's sitting upright in her seat, a look of disbelief and shock on her face. Her mascara is running down her cheeks. She looks like a porcelain mime doll – though perhaps one that's slightly melting. She's holding her left arm tightly to her side.

"Hey, you okay?" I manage. My voice comes out through what feels like a clogged throat.

"I think so," she says, still staring straight into the bright white, snow-caked windshield.

Bright-white! It's day time. I bolt upright in my seat and my ribs and stomach scream in agony. Yep, I may have broken something. I just cringe and lean back into the seat to cower in the fear of daylight.

We're wanted. I don't know where we are. And it's the middle of the day. No cloak of night to hide us from the boogeyman. Anyone could be right outside these coated windows and we would know nothing about it.

"Jace?" Carly says. She leans towards me, but winces and grasps her arm more tightly.

"I'm not even sure what happened," I say. "I'm so sorry."

"Don't do that. I'm going to need you to keep that famous cool of yours. It's not your fault."

"Shit! I just didn't see the curve in time."

Speaking, even breathing, hurts. I feel it deep in my ribs and chest.

"Calm down. What hurts?"

"My ribs," I say. "I'm fine. Just give me a minute. Are-are you okay?"

"My arm hurts," she says. "I don't think it's broken though. I can move it a little. It's just really not a good idea."

"Remember what you said about snow covering us up?" I say. "I hope you were right. We'll just have to lay low for a while, hope no one finds us, and try our damndest not to freeze to death."

"Good plan. I think we could manage to stay warm if we weren't all busted up," Carly winces.

"Flirting at a time like this? You've changed, Carly. I must be a bad influence."

"Oh, shut up!" she laughs.

I stop laughing and fall into an uncharacteristic silence.

"I didn't mean that literally," Carly says through a sarcastic, yet wincing, smile.

"No. Shh!" I say. "I think I heard something outside."

We both freeze. I can hear a steady hum of light wind rushing around the car, but little else.

"I guess it's just my imagination," I say.

A few hours pass, presumably. Mal's battery is once again not cooperating, along with most of her other functions. Neither one of us really say much, just sit there and watch the blinding white layer of snow on the windshield gradually get duller and duller.

"Jace, had you ever thought about me before? Like as a girlfriend, I mean?" Carly finally says.

She is curled up into the seat with her back up against the door. She's nursing her arm by holding it steady against her chest.

"What? Well, no. I guess not. We always just had fun together, you know?"

"Yeah, I know," she says. "So why now?"

I don't say anything. Not at first. I consider my options. Lie or not to lie, that is the question, I suppose. I look at Carly and she doesn't deserve a lie. She deserves the truth, because anything I say to her could indeed be the last thing. But I guess that's true for anyone if you really think about it.

"Honestly, I had never thought of any girl seriously before. I dated a few girls, sure. You know that. But I had never thought, 'what if I spent the rest of my life with her,' or something like that. But you, well, I don't want to die with the regret of never having you as more than a friend. Or at least trying to, you know."

"Jace, you're not going to die. You're…"

She stops dead and if her complexion consisted of very much color at all, I'm sure it would have drained out just now. She looks like a young child who just placed the last piece to her jigsaw puzzle only to realize it's a detailed picture of a slaughterhouse.

"Remember my little problem," I say, thumbing my nose and then mimicking an explosion with my hands and mouth. BOOM!

"Oh shit. Did you go to the doctor?"

I can't even bring myself to answer verbally. I just shake my head no.

"Why the fuck not? If you honestly think you could die any day now, why would you not go?"

"Because if I have two weeks left as we speak, I'm sure the doctor's would cut that in half with all their bullshit tests and treatments. Not to mention, the little time I have left would be completely miserable!"

"You don't know that!"

"Yeah, well my Aunt Winnie does."

Carly opens her mouth to speak, but doesn't.

"Look, the bottom line is, if I have two weeks or 20 years left, I want to spend them with you. It just took a little crisis to make me grow up enough to know it."

"I'm..." She thumbs at a loose thread on the seat upholstery. "I'm not sure if that's sweet or not. I think it is."

I can't help but laugh, and thankfully, she smiles. "I meant it to be," I say.

I lean forward, wincing as the pain quickly returns to my abdomen. I ignore it as best I can and lean far across the console and kiss Carly's lips. They're cold, and still taste faintly of black licorice. Taste be damned, I'm still grateful for that kiss, and I hold onto it until the pain in my gut becomes too much.

"You're amazing," I say.

"Aww, you're going to make me blush," she says.

"By all means, please blush," I say, hugging myself tightly. "Anything to keep the blood flowing."

Another silent moment passes.

"What do you think it's like to die?" Carly says.

I start to answer right away, but I stumble. This actually deserves a bit of thought.

After brief contemplation, I say: "I think it's sort of like going to sleep. You'd be sitting there having a thought, and then there's nothing. You probably wouldn't even know if you were asleep or dead until you woke up – or well, didn't."

"That sort of makes me want to be an insomniac," she says through a slight smile.

"It sort of makes me less scared to die."

19

Eventually, I drift off to sleep while just watching Carly. A month ago, I would have felt very creepy watching a girl this long, especially while she's falling to sleep herself. But not now. Not Carly.

It's dark when I wake up, the blinding glare on the windshield completely gone. Carly is still asleep, and I can't help but smile and feel a little giddy when I look at her.

The wind is still bustling around outside, so I hone in on the sound and try to imagine what sort of frigid landscape surrounds us. The sound is oddly relaxing. I'm about to drift off when I realize I really need to take a piss.

Now, if you've never been snowed inside a crashed car while being chased by a drunken, violence-prone maniac and the police, let me be the first to tell you: where to piss is a bit of an issue. I look at Carly sleeping and consider pissing inside an empty bottle, provided I can find one.

No luck though. Not an empty bottle in sight. And maybe the pee is going to my brain, or I just heard a voice.

I stop rummaging around the vehicle and settle back into my seat, clutching my stomach as though trying to hold my guts inside. Silence. Wind. A voice!

"Oh shit. Carly." I nudge her knee gently. "Carly, wake up!"

She stirs slightly and rubs her eyes with her left hand.

"What's up?" she says.

"I think we have a visitor, dear."

We both sit silently now, holding our breath and waiting. And there it is again, a voice. I can't make out what they're saying, but it comes in short bursts of loud speech. I can't make out who it is, but it sounds like a man's voice.

Dear God, please, please, please don't let it be Carly's dad. Cops be damned, jail is better than both of us dying out here in the woods.

Hopefully, we're buried so far beneath a mountain of snow that the car will simply look like a small hill. But I doubt it.

"You hear that, right?" I ask Carly, just confirming that I'm not completely insane.

"Yes! What the hell are we going to do?" she whispers.

"I suppose there's always the chance they don't notice us."

Carly looked at me as if I had just suggested we get out and dance naked.

"Okay, maybe not," I say. "I see two options. Lock the doors and turtle up or run for it."

I say this, but I'm not even sure I can run. I may have broken a rib when Mal took her fateful plunge. It hurts to even sit up.

Carly looks like she's about to say something, hopefully brilliant because I am completely out of ideas, but she is interrupted by a heavy thump at the driver's side window – someone rapping at our frigid shell no doubt. Just a thin layer of ice stands between us and Carly's dad, the police or maybe (though unlikely) even worse horrors.

"We have to go now," I say, and reach across Carly's lap to unlock the passenger door and pop it open. She gets out quickly and I scramble across the console, pain searing in my side the whole time, and follow.

We hobble into the darkness like two wounded animals. The snow is much deeper than I expected. Each footfall reminds me that my tennis shoes weren't exactly made for tundra travel. Snow spills into my shoes and bites at the soles of my feet, threatening to creep down to my toes.

As we sat huddled in the car, I didn't picture that the air outside could be much colder, but man was I wrong. The wind bites at my face and the snow soaks my shoes and socks, making me long for the frigid air and crisp, cold leather surface of Mal's interior.

The snow is still coming down hard. There must be at least eight inches on the ground. I can barely see Carly running in front of me and the pain in my ribs makes it difficult to catch up, or run, or breathe. Adrenaline, don't fail me now!

Trees, snow and darkness. It's all a blur and I'm struggling to force each foot to take another step. All I can hear is wind and crunching footfalls, but I can't tell if we're being chased. And honestly, I'm afraid to look back.

The trees ahead are growing denser. I figure we had better avoid the thickest of it, so I call, "Carly!" Again, "Carly! This way!" It's now that I realize Carly is nowhere in sight. Here I stand alone with the cold, the snow and the crazy person who chased us out of the car. No, wait. No crazy person in sight.

Does that mean he went after Carly? Shit!

I turn in all directions trying to catch a glimpse of any kind of movement. Nothing. Okay, Jace, old boy, do *not* panic. But I think it's too late.

I trudge off into the blackness to find Carly, hopefully, before our would-be captor does.

I haven't taken more than ten steps when I hear someone shouting in the distance. I can't quite make it out.

It sounds like they're calling someone's name, and I can just understand it enough to know that it's not mine.

It sounds like, "Aaah-Eeee!"

I strain my hearing to its fucking limits, trying to hear through the howling wind and rustling branches.

"Arr-Lee!"

Carly? Whoever that is hasn't found her yet. And I can't be sure out here – everything sounds and looks so surreal – but it doesn't sound much like her dad. From what little I've heard of him.

I try to hone in on that voice and move towards it. Hell, for all I know I may be heading in the complete opposite direction. But damn it, I should get an A for effort. I walk slowly and each time the voice calls out again I try to tell if it's closer or farther away.

But it has to be closer now. I can hear it so much clearer than before. As a matter of fact, the source of the voice is right upon me before I notice it isn't saying "Carly" at all.

"Harvey!" the voice calls from right behind me.

20

I jump and spin around to see a vaguely familiar face. I try to say something profound, but it's so hard to breathe. All that comes out is, "What the fuck?"

"Harvey, calm down," she says.

"Emily?" I say, complete with air-finger quotes.

"Yeah, it's me," she says, reaching her hand out to me. "Just calm down. I'm not here to hurt you or Carly."

I just look at her, trying to put this puzzle together, but I believe a few pieces have slid under the couch, maybe even down the air vent.

"Where is she?" she says.

"I don't know," I gasp. "She was right… right in front of me. But I lost her. Couldn't keep. Keep up. Think I may have broken a rib."

"Let's find her. Hurry!" she says and extends her hand even further. I take it and we trudge on to search for Carly.

I let Emily do most of the calling out. She repeats, "Carly! Carly!" over and over again every few feet, while helping me to trudge along with her.

"Hey! There!" I say, pointing at a lump on the ground. The lump is quickly gathering snow and it wouldn't be long before it is covered completely.

Emily and I move towards it and I almost collapse when I realize I'm right. It's Carly, slumped motionless on the ground.

I kneel down beside her and gather her in my arms.

"Shit. Oh man, oh shit. What are we going to do?" I say, oblivious to the pain in my side.

Emily kneels down with her and checks Carly's pulse.

"She's alive. But we have to get out of this storm or we won't be for long!"

"We need to get her to a hospital!" I shout, only realizing after I said it that it could mean falling right into the hands of the police or even Carly's dad. But that doesn't matter. If Carly is hurt, she needs help. And police be damned, maybe they can protect Carly from her dad. After all, her birthday is only 10 days away.

"I don't think the car will go anywhere in this," Emily says. "Assuming that we could even make it back up to the road."

"Then what?"

"This way," Emily says. "We have to get out of this and warm up. I think I saw just the place earlier when I was out here looking for you guys."

"Looking for us? What?" I say.

"This way!"

We both shoulder Carly's weight and I let Emily take the lead. At this point, I don't have much of a choice. We keep going, stomping through snow that is only getting deeper. I don't even look up, just let Emily – consciously I know that's not her real name, I remember – guide me into the night. I just hope she has a genius fucking plan in mind that doesn't end with me behind bars and / or Carly dead.

Suddenly, my feet stop crunching upon heavy snow and instead land flat and solid against hard wood. I look up and the three of us are standing on a dark porch that I didn't even see coming. Emily thumps on the door with the heel of her hand, waits a few moments, then thumps again.

"I don't think anyone is home," she says. "But we have to get in. We have to get warm and check on Carly."

She moves further down the porch, leaving all of Carly's weight on my shoulder, and begins fumbling with a window.

Finally, I can be of use.

I dig into my back pocket and retrieve my wallet, and then awkwardly open it and pull my learners' permit out with my teeth. Still holding Carly up, I drop the wallet and place the permit in between the door and enjambment. A few flicks and a little bit of pressure and the door swings open.

"Hey," I say. "Got it."

Emily hurries down to the door and together we help Carly inside and shut the door behind us. It's pitch black. I try the light switch beside the door, but nothing happens.

"Looks like the power's out."

"Let's find somewhere to put Carly down and I'll try to find a lamp or something," Emily says.

We fumble through the darkness of the unfamiliar cabin and find what feels to be a couch and ease Carly down onto it. Emily goes to look for something to light the room up and I slump down by Carly's side and drape one arm over her.

***

The next thing I know, I'm waking up and the room is glowing a dull orange. At first, I have no fucking clue where I am or what is going on. Is the strange building on fire? No, I think not.

"She's going to be okay," Emily says. She's lounged back in a rustic arm chair that is draped with a tattered quilt, puffing on a cigarette.

"What happened? How long was I out?"

"You were only out about a half hour," she says. "And as for Carly, it looks like she took a fall and hit her head." She motions to Carly's forehead where a small, plum-colored bump has formed.

"Holy shit!" I say, burying my face in my hands. "I just realized I have so many damned questions I don't even know where to start."

"Pick one," Emily says.

"Okay. Who are you, really? How do you know Carly's name? How did you find us?"

"That's technically three questions. But those are good ones. May take a bit of explaining. First, I know Carly's name the same way I know yours, Jace."

"Then why shout 'Harvey' in the woods? That's the fake ass name I gave you when we were hitchhiking."

"Well, I tried shouting your real name back at the rest stop. That didn't seem to work. So I figured I would use the fake one, hoping you'd put two and two together and realize I wasn't a threat."

"That was you at the rest stop?" Now that she mentions it, I can totally see it. I just imagine her from a distance and through the filthy bathroom window. Yep, that's our stalker!

She looks so much different than I remember from our little hitchhiking experiment. Her coat is off now. She's wearing a purple blouse and gray slacks. Very professional. She doesn't look like the do-gooder Samaritan I had pegged her for.

"I've been trying to find you kids for days. Ever since you ran off. Stupid idea, by the way. But I think I know why you did it."

"Are you a cop?" I ask.

"No! Now, shush and let me finish. I've been trying to find you because I'm on your side, believe it or not. I'm a social worker. I've been investigating Carly's father over alleged child abuse. We hadn't been able to prove anything yet, and things were really just getting started. But I knew enough not to believe the bullshit he was spouting to the police about you kidnapping Carly."

"Glad I don't have to defend myself to you, I guess. I'm trying to help. That's all."

"Why didn't you go to the police?" Emily asks.

"I guess I've seen too much TV. I figured at worst they wouldn't believe us. Or at best, they couldn't do anything without a proper investigation, which could put Carly in a dangerous spot. She turns 18 in just a few days, so I figured we would just take off until then. Then she could do whatever she wanted. Not have to live with him anymore, you know?"

"I get it. Still, you both could have been killed. Or if Carly's father had found you first... Well, I don't even want to think about that."

"That makes two of us."

"I just want you kids to be safe. And I'll do whatever I can to make sure Carly is never abused again."

"Well, there's only, what? 10 more days until she's 18. No problem. If we can just hold out a few more days, everything will be alright."

Emily, or whatever her name is, takes another drag from her cigarette.

I get to my feet and look around, realizing that the hard floor didn't do my ribs any favors. I wince and clutch my side, but still have enough wits about me to realize Emily had lit a fire in a fireplace I didn't even know was there. I suppose that would explain why I'm not still freezing my ass off.

"You ok?" Emily asks.

"I think I may have cracked a rib or something. Not sure. I'll be okay though."

I sit down on the couch next to Carly and stroke her hair.

"Hold on," I say, having a startlingly brilliant moment of clarity. "You were even following us back when we were hitchhiking, weren't you?"

"Not following you, exactly," she says. "I had heard about what happened that night with Carly's father and wanted to look a little deeper. I didn't know exactly where you disappeared to after the altercation, but I had an idea."

She gets to her feet and walks over to me.

"Why don't you clean yourself up and get some rest? Hopefully, the snow will slack off by morning and we can get to a hospital."

"Okay, yeah. Just..." Damn stammering. "Just don't let him get to her. Please."

She places her hand on my shoulder and says, "You have my word."

21

Maybe I shouldn't, but I can't help wonder whose cabin this is. It's a rustic old place. Not rotting and falling down, but dusty, even saw-dusty.

I've settled on the first bedroom I came to once I left the living room. The place isn't very big after all: a living room, a kitchenish looking thing, bathroom, a short hallway and two bedrooms. At least, that's all I've seen.

Carly is in the other bedroom, Emily on the couch in the living room: our only defense against whatever comes through the front door.

I pull back the blanket and sheets on the bed and dust puffs up into the air. A musty smell assaults my nostrils, reminiscent of the blanket at the bottom of the stack in Grandma's closet. Regretfully, I climb into the large, filthy bed still wearing my shoes.

The room is scary dark. I ease onto my back and stare up into it, waiting for sleep. The bed may be filthy, but it is much better than the floor. I ponder the worst. Carly's dad could come crashing through the front door, or even a window, any minute. Then all of this would have been for nothing.

I feel so incredibly stupid right now. I fucked up. Fucked up bad. My intentions were golden, of course. But those intentions have led Carly and I here.

Let's do the list. Car wreck, check. Injuries for both of us, check. Nearly froze to death in a blizzard, check. Stuck in a strange, possibly haunted, cabin with a stranger who claims to want nothing but the best for us, check.

This all reeks of stupidity, and I fear it was my stupidity that led us here.

Maybe if I can get to sleep, I'll dream about smarter things. Simpler times. Non-broken bones.

***

"Jace! Wake up!" I hear this hushed whisper as I slowly drift back to consciousness.

I can't see her, but I know it's Carly. The bed shifts, as she sits on the edge.

"Hey, what's up?" I say.

"Shhh!" she hisses. "Keep it down."

"Okay, yeah. Sorry. What's wrong?" I say in a barely audible whisper.

"I thought I heard something outside. It's probably just the storm, but it still freaked me out."

I strain my ears to see if I can hear anything odd, but it's all rustling branches, howling wind and the occasional creak of the old cabin.

"Yeah, it's probably just the storm," I say. "You want to sleep in here?"

"I'm not sure a social worker will take too kindly to her 17-year-old subject crawling into bed with her boyfriend under her watch."

"Baby, if you were a subject, I would never stop studying."

"Damnit! You're so corny. If your ribs weren't crushed I would probably fuck you stupid right now."

"The feeling is mutual," I say. "Can we just cuddle instead? It's warmer and good for the ribs."

"Scootch."

She crawls into bed with me, and I can tell even in the darkness that she's still favoring her arm. It could be broken, which reminds me that I should hate myself even more than I already do.

Carly slides perfectly into place, right next to me. I hold her gently, remaining weary of her arm.

After a few minutes of silence, she whispers, "Do you think my dad could follow our foot prints?"

"What?" I say, half asleep.

"The prints we made in the snow when we came here. Do you think he can find us because of that?"

I think for a moment. "I doubt it. The snow was really coming down out there. Our prints are probably covered up by now."

"Yeah, you're probably right." I can tell she's nervous as hell. Even at a whisper, I can hear her voice quivering.

"Try not to worry. Everything will be okay."

"Yeah."

I can feel sleep taking me. The dark is getting darker, and thoughts are fading.

But a loud thump, no a bang, jolts me back awake. Carly jerks and sits up in bed. I can feel her trembling.

"What the hell was that?" she says.

"I'm not sure."

I no more than get those words out before we hear it again, louder this time. I can also hear a muffled voice.

"Shit, someone is outside."

I sit up quickly and throw my legs over the edge of the bed, trying desperately to ignore the pain in my ribs. The fire in the living room had warmed the place up quite a bit, but it was still cold enough that I went to bed with my coat on. Thankfully, Carly did too.

I creep to the door and peek out. The living room is a dull orange, faintly lit by the dying fire in the fireplace. Emily is standing in front of the door.

"Hey, what the hell is that?" I say.

"Not sure, but it doesn't sound friendly."

"We need to get out of here," I say, still trying to keep my voice down. "Now!"

"I wonder if this place has a back door," Carly says, suddenly standing next to me.

Again, a loud thump followed by an angry, muffled voice. Then the thump gives way to pounding over and over again.

My stomach is tying in knots and my knees feel so weak they will barely hold me up. I need to run from a madman and I feel like shit. Just my luck.

"You two see if you can find a way outside, and I'll try to deal with him." It's Carly's dad. I know it and Emily knows it. Carly likely knows it too. "With any luck I can make him believe this is my cabin and I don't even know who Carly is."

"No offense, but that sounds insane," I say. "He will probably just beat your ass and then ours. We either run like hell, or barricade the doors and windows."

Emily thinks about this for a moment. I turn to ask Carly her thoughts, but she is no longer standing beside me. Shit! Where did she go?

"We would probably stand a better chance in here than out in the storm. Help me barricade the door!"

We each grab a corner of the worn couch and start shoving. The old thing is heavy as hell, and it makes a terrible scraping noise as we inch it closer to the door. A few more heaves, busted ribs be damned, and it sits firmly against the heavy front door. It's now that I notice the pounding has stopped.

I put my ear up against the door, but hear nothing.

"Is he gone?" Emily says.

"Either gone, frozen to death or went to find another way in. Where the hell is Carly?"

We both hurry back to the hallway, the last place I saw Carly.

"Carly!" Calling her name so quietly into the darkness feels futile, but I do it any way. "Carly!"

"Jace, in here!" she says. "I found something."

Please be a gun. Please be a gun. Please be a gun.

I walk into the other bedroom, not the one I was sleeping in, and can barely make her out, standing in the dark corner of the room.

"What is it?" I say.

"We need to get out of here!" Emily says from the hallway. "This crazy bastard is trying to break the window, and I don't think it will take him long."

I can hear it. The sound of something repeatedly smacking the cold glass of the cabin window.

"Up here!" Carly says. "I found an attic."

As my eyes adjust little by little, I see that she is standing next to an old wooden ladder that she had pulled down from the ceiling.

"There's a pretty good chance he won't find us up here. I found it purely by luck while looking for a way out."

"Sounds good. Let's go!" I say.

Carly clambers up the ladder as quickly as her injured arm will allow. I follow, and then Emily.

Emily and I struggle to lift the heavy combination of ladder and door back up to be flush with the ceiling, and eventually succeed.

The attic is pitch dark and smells like old, dead things. I imagine that the three of us are sitting amidst a room of decaying corpses, rats, shit and God knows what else. But most likely, it's just mold and mustiness from years of non-use.

I hear glass breaking down below. He's inside! Carly nestles close to me and I cradle her inside my arms. We shrink back into the darkness.

Carly and I are shaking so hard, I can't tell if it's me, her or both of us.

Hopefully, he'll break in, act like a drunken idiot, notice no one is home, and leave.

I can hear his voice booming. "Carly! You here? Carly!" For a moment, I almost feel bad for him. His voice sounds drenched in worry. But then I remember what he's done.

He has to know we're here, right? I mean, at least that someone was here at some point. For Christ's sake, there's still a fire going! But all we can do is wait, huddled in the dank attic, freezing, shaking, hoping.

Footsteps pound those old creaky floorboards below us. They get louder, then softer, and then louder again. I can feel my heart speeding up and slowing down in sequence with those footsteps and the awful fate they're sure to bring.

Oh fuck us! Two innocent kids huddled in an attic from a would-be murderer, sure-as-shit child abuser. We don't deserve this.

Emily doesn't seem as scared as us on the surface, but I swear I can feel her shaking in the darkness. Sure, she's an adult. But what the hell is she going to do against Carly's dad? The man is a walking, talking monster – something straight out of Universal, no Hammer Horror film.

Finally, the footsteps get softer and softer, until eventually they are gone. I listen intently, but all I can hear is the stilted sound of my breathing and possibly Carly's bones knocking together. An unsteady breeze gusting through a hallway full of skeletons.

"I think he's gone," Emily says.

I hold my breath and listen, swearing to myself that it's too good to be true. Sure enough, I hear nothing. But I think I smell something.

"Do you guys smell smoke?" I say.

"Yes," Emily says. "And the fire in the living room was almost out, so I don't think it's coming from there."

"Oh shit!" Carly says. "We have to get out of here!"

Carly lowers the attic door and a raging orange glow invades the dark of the attic, accompanied by strong heat that abolishes the cold.

The sick fuck set the cabin on fire.

Luckily – strange word to use in our current predicament – the flames haven't reached the bedroom yet, but I can see them licking everything in the living room.

All that licking… The word "kinky" comes to mind, but I force it away due to the severity of the situation.

We scramble down the ladder like a pack of sewer rats running from 10,000 flushing toilets. Emily heads for the door, but the flames are in the hallway.

"Shit!" she screams.

I often suffer moments of clarity during emergencies. This time, I find myself straining for this clarity and finding nothing.

I scan the room, the walls, the door, the bed. Is there a way out? There fucking has to be!

Walls. Walls have windows. Windows have curtains. Curtains hide windows and windows break. I look for curtains and… bingo!

I pull the curtains from their hanger, which clatters to the floor along with the curtains.

"This way!" I shout above the sound of raging fire and coughing females. I try to open the window but it doesn't budge. I check and double check the lock but it's already open. And without a thought, I step back and run full force at the window, bound a single foot off the bed and hurl myself through it.

Everything is hot, then cold, then stinging. I thud against the ground and familiar arms cradle me. The familiar warm embrace of my own blood.

22

"Oh shit!" I hear Carly scream as she clambers out the window and drops to the ground. Within seconds she's by my side.

"Is he okay?" Emily says.

"I seriously doubt it. He has this problem. When he bleeds, sometimes he doesn't stop. And I don't know what to do."

Carly is clearly panicking, as am I. My heart is about to pump out of my chest, which is extra bad at the moment, since that means increased blood flow. And that blood isn't confined to my veins. It has several new exits – not just the nose this time – all created by my little trip through the window.

I start to speak, but Carly's scream startles me so bad the words get stuck in my throat. Suddenly, she's not beside me anymore. I strain to raise myself to my elbows only to see her being dragged away by her dad.

He has a fistful of her hair and she's screaming as her heels make fresh trenches in the snow.

I force myself up to my knees and a fresh drop of blood runs the length of my nose, bulbs at the end for a moment, before falling to dot the snow.

"Hey! You fuck!" I scream, hardly recognizing my own voice. "Stop!"

He actually stops. Surprising, I know. When he looks at me, I quickly scan the area to locate Emily. She and I will need to stand together against this monster. Unfortunately, all I find is her motionless body crumpled in the snow.

Well, shit.

He's coming towards me mumbling something. I fumble around in the snow and come up with a piece of broken window, a fine weapon for a fellow with a clotting disorder.

I take it into my bare hand and charge my pursuer. He brushes me away with a single stroke and I roll to the ground, still clutching my piece of glass.

I crawl and scrape and finally get back to my feet, this time standing firmly – well, not firmly, but determined nonetheless – between Carly and her father. I feel blood running down my face and neck, down my hands and dripping from the tips of my fingers. I pant and gasp for air, and a crimson mist spews from my lips with each exhale.

Hemogoblin to the rescue!

This is the time when super powers would really come in handy. I feel intimidating, oozing blood from every orifice. But Carly's dad is unrelenting, not intimidated in the slightest.

He comes at me again and I swing my glass wide, hoping to connect. Nothing. I back away and steady myself.

The world is whirling around me and my legs feel like gelatin. I close my eyes and slash again, hoping. This time the glass gashes his stomach and he bellows a mad cry.

A moment of hope invades me. He can bleed. If he can bleed, I can put him down. I have to! The problem is that I can bleed to. In fact, I'm better at it than he is. Which sucks. He hits me again, this time square in the face and I feel my nose crunch beneath the weight of his fist, a fresh burst of red sprays the snow as I land flat on my back.

I can hear Carly whimpering behind me, begging and pleading for her dad to stop. She's crying and scared and I'm fucking powerless to do anything about it.

She cradles my head in her lap. It feels familiar and good. I breathe it in and enjoy this moment. I want to make it last forever, and so help me God, if I could I would freeze time and live here in this frozen wasteland, head in Carly's lap, for all eternity. Because familiar and good are both things I can live with.

I expect him to drag me away from his daughter at any moment, to finish me off and return for her. He'll probably kill her too, and leave our bodies as a crimson, abstract art that dissipates with each falling snowflake.

An enormous crack fills the sky and seems to echo off every tree. Carly's dad's face grows distant and his determined stride drops to one knee, then both knees, before his bearded, hideous face lands next to me in the snow.

Behind him stands our savior, Emily, holding a small handgun in a still trembling hand.

23

Snow and cold become black and nothing, and the next thing I know I'm lying in a hospital bed under pale, white lights. For just a moment, I think I'm dead and those white lights are Heaven's gates glowing in the sun.

Then I smell that old familiar stench, the aggressive, intrusive Sweet Annie herself – and I know they wouldn't allow that bitch into Heaven. Or me for that matter.

I see Carly standing next to me, her arm in a sling, her hair clean and fresh make-up applied, her lips glowing a pretty plum color, which unfortunately smells and tastes like literal shit.

I love her anyway.

"Hey," I say, finding it surprisingly difficult to speak.

"Hey," she says, and gently strokes the blankets that cover my legs. "How are you feeling?"

I take a moment to assess the situation so I can provide an honest answer.

"Do you remember when we were in eighth grade? Jordan Reynolds found a dead cat in the school's swimming pool. Then he got it out and chased you and Alan with it. Remember that?"

She nods her head and a tear rolls from her left eye.

"Well, I feel like that cat looked, only a more dull, drugged version of it."

Carly smiles and pulls a chair to my bedside. She sits and lays her head on my shoulder.

"I can't remember who screamed louder, you or Alan," I chuckle.

"Hey buddy. I heard that!" Alan said, peeking his head through the door. "The doc said you were sedated but coming around, said we could poke in and see you for a minute before letting you rest for the night."

"Oh man, it's good to see you," I say. My voice sounds like a rusted pop can rattling against bicycle spokes.

"Same here!" he says. "I was worried sick about you guys. When you stopped calling, I knew it had all gone to shit."

Mom and Emily come through the door and suddenly I'm surrounded by nothing but friends. It feels too good to be true. Then I wonder if it is.

"Jace! What were you thinking?" Mom gasps. "You had me worried sick. Oh, God! I'm just so glad you're alright."

She kneels next to me and kisses me on top of my head. Tears are streaming down her face and those tears remind me how much my little stunt hurt the people I love.

"I love you!" Mom says.

"I love you too."

Salty tears begin to well up in my eyes and it burns, deservingly so.

"So, like, am I going to jail or anything?" I say. "For kidnapping or whatever that bullshit was?"

"No, Jace," Emily says. "Carly and I explained everything to the authorities. They all agree, myself included, that what you and Carly did was stupid, ill-timed and immature, but that your heart was in the right place."

"Stupid? Immature?" I say through a forced grin. "What do you expect? We're teenagers." I strain to laugh a bit, but it quickly turns into a hacking cough.

"I don't know what I would have done without you," Carly says. "People can say what they want. I'm lucky that you're my friend, my boyfriend, someone who would stand up for me when no one else would."

"I know you'd do the same for me," I say. "As a matter of fact, you did. More times than I can count."

She smiles, and that smile is worth my weight in money.

"What happened to your dad?" I ask, remembering the gruesome scene we left behind in the snow.

Emily starts to speak, but Carly interrupts.

"He's dead."

I lean forward and take her pale hand in both of my heavily bandaged ones. I know the man beat her senseless, may have even killed her if given the opportunity. But he was still her dad, something I never knew.

"I'm okay," she whispers.

"And what happens to you?" I say without giving much thought to how it sounds.

"Carly will be staying with us for a while, honey." Mom says. "She'll be 18 in a few days so there's no need for any foster family crap. Then when you all are ready, you can move out, or hang around for a few years. Either way is fine with me."

"Thanks, Mom."

She smiles at me. The most genuine smile I've seen from her in years.

"Emily, you saved our lives, and I still don't even know your real name," I say. "You know what, I think Emily will do. Emily saved us and that's who I want to remember."

She smiles.

I barely have time to appreciate this room full of awesome people before the doctor comes in – a tall, thin man with receding brown hair and a full, healthy beard.

"Okay, folks. Let's let him get some rest. You can all come back tomorrow, and if he continues to improve we can move him out of the ICU."

Everyone says their goodbyes, offers hugs and kisses and heart-felt well wishes, and then they're heading for the door.

"Hey guys, could I have just one more moment alone with Carly?" I say. "I won't be long. Promise."

"Sure," the doctor says. "But let's make it quick. You need your rest."

I nod as he leaves the room with everyone else.

"Carly," I say. "I love you so much. Friend, lover, partner in crime. You get an A+ in all these categories. Five stars. For sure."

"I know," she says. "Especially the partner in crime bit, I should hope."

We both laugh, which sounds off and foreign in the otherwise empty hospital room.

"You know, I swore I would never end up here," I say, gazing around the stark, white place. "Everything is so sanitary and smelly at the same time. You can tell they're trying so hard to cover up the smell of the last person who died in here."

"Let's be real," Carly says. "It's a good thing you are in here. You're stable right now. You weren't out in the snow. You were bleeding out quick." Her voice cracks and she covers her mouth with her hand, the nails painted a fresh coat of black. "Hopefully, the doctor can tell us what's wrong with you by morning and get you started on treatment. I don't plan on letting you die any time soon. We have a life ahead of us. College. Work. Apartments." She lowers her voice. "And more sex!"

"Lots of sex," I say and grin.

But Carly doesn't chuckle. She's trembling.

"Hey," I say. "I'm not going to die. I'm going to be fine. Smile for me. You know I love that smile."

She forces a smile through a veil of tears and it's still one of the most beautiful things I've ever seen in my life.

"Besides," I say, "I wouldn't dare let you renege on the 'lots of sex' part."

This brings on an inexorable chuckle.

"You always know how to make me laugh," she says. "You always have."

The doctor reappears in the doorway.

"Excuse me, miss. It's time to go. He'll be here tomorrow." He offers a slight smile and leaves the room.

"I'll see you tomorrow," I say. "Now, kiss me. Kiss me like you fucking mean it."

And she does!

The taste is dreadful, but the pressure of her soft lips on mine is purely divine.

"I love you too," she whispers, before kissing me once again on my forehead. She exits the room, leaving behind the taste and smell of foul, back licorice.

I lick my lips, and so help me, it actually isn't as bad as I remember. Maybe my taste buds are growing up, changing with me. Or maybe it's just time I start associating the simple things in life with happier times.

I give my lips one final lick and remember the fullness of Carly's lips, the warmth of her body. My head drifts to a happy place, one where Carly and I have a life of our own in a tiny, one-bedroom apartment. Maybe we'll have a cat. Maybe a dog. She'll go to college and do her thing. I'll do my thing, whatever that is. We'll love each other the way people are supposed to. Not the way most people actually do.

I can see it now: long Saturday afternoons spent eating pizza and marathoning our favorite movies, right there on the living room floor. Probably naked. Well, preferably naked.

She'll never feel pain at the hands of a loved one again. I'll see to it. She'll feel warmth and kindness, because she deserves those things. She'll always know that I'm there for her, like sun in the summer or leaves in the fall. And I'll always know that she is there for me. We'll spend our lives waiting for the next...

END

www.ingramcontent.com/pod-product-compliance
Lightning Source LLC
Chambersburg PA
CBHW030230180626
46810CB00008B/3060